INFILTRATION

BOOK ONE OF THE AFTER DARK SERIES

Visit us at www.boldstrokesbooks.com

INFILTRATION

BOOK ONE OF THE AFTER DARK SERIES

by

Jackie D

2015

INFILTRATION

ISBN 13: 978-1-62639-521-3

THIS TRADE PAPERBACK ORIGINAL IS PUBLISHED BY
BOLD STROKES BOOKS, INC.
P.O. BOX 249
VALLEY FALLS, NY 12185

FIRST EDITION: DECEMBER 2015

CREDITS
EDITORS: VICTORIA VILLASENOR AND CINDY CRESAP
PRODUCTION DESIGN: STACIA SEAMAN
COVER DESIGN BY GABRIELLE PENDERGRAST

Acknowledgments

Looking back on the process of creating this story, the number of people involved is endless. First and foremost, thank you to everyone at Bold Strokes Books for letting me share this story with the world. Vic Villasenor, thank you for your patience, insight, and brilliant editing. Cindy Cresap, for noticing everything else that we missed. Thank you to everyone behind the scenes that worked to bring all of these characters to the readers. I feel incredibly privileged to be a part of such an amazing group of people. Thank you to the wonderful friends in my life: Stacy, Debbie, Audra, Tina, Christina, and my sister Julie, who all read draft after draft, always willing to give their insight and ask questions. Thank you to my unbelievably supportive girlfriend Alexis, who always pushes me to write more, create more, and be better. Finally, to everyone else that has supported me through this very exciting, sometimes frustrating, but always rewarding process, thank you. I love you all.

For my mom. A few words will never be enough thanks for everything you have given me, but it's a start. I love you.

CHAPTER ONE

*T*he smell of blood filled her senses, copper permeating her world.

"Gunnery Sergeant! Gunnery Sergeant!" The call came in, bellowing over the radio. Tyler strained to reach for it over the bodies...the bodies of her team, her friends, people she trusted and who trusted her. The roadside bomb had gone off without warning, and as she looked around, her head still ringing, vision blurry, she realized there was no feeling in her left side, but she had been the only one spared.

Her hand shook as she brought the radio closer, the wires exposed and the plastic burnt, still warm. How it was still working was beyond her comprehension. "Alpha team down, need medevac. Location is two klicks east of primary target."

The response was broken, but she was sure she could hear "Roger that, Top."

She pushed the debris clear from her legs, only to discover that her left leg had a protruding bone right below her knee. "Fuck me." She crawled to each of her teammates as the acid burned the back of her throat, and she checked pulses for signs of life. She knew it was fruitless, done out of ingrained training more than rational thought. Blood oozed from her ear and dizziness set in. Just before everything went black, she saw a uniform running toward her. The red cross strapped to his arm filled her vision, and then everything went black.

Tyler's eyes flew open, and she pushed herself upright, sweat running between her shoulder blades and down her chest. Her breathing was erratic, and she looked around the hotel room to assure herself it wasn't the desert of Iraq. She managed a quiet and broken "Damn it." A quick glance at the bedside clock confirmed the internal one that was always ticking: 3:18 a.m. She swung her legs over the side of the bed and rubbed her face in the darkness, needing to feel something that grounded her in this plane of existence. The screams were always there, always lingering right beneath the surface. *Why can't I get away?*

She shuffled into the bathroom and turned on the shower. There was no way she was going to get back to sleep, and she had to report to a new assignment. With her arms propped on the sink, she stared at the mirror, closing her eyes tightly for a moment and then slowly opening them, in some way hoping to erase all the nightmares. It had never worked before, and she knew this morning would be no different. The memories clung to her subconscious like newly developed scabs that begged to be scratched. Her eyes mirrored the pain of where she had been, what she had seen, and the things she had done. She resolved to push it to the back of her mind, as she always did when these moments crept up on her. She let the spray flow over her face, silently hoping that the water would cling to some of the wounds and drag them down the drain.

❖

Brooke Hart made her way down the long corridors of Camp Peary toward the dining hall. It was the first day of her final segment of training at "The Farm," and she had to admit she was excited. Although her expertise was in computer surveillance, all agents were required to take a six-week course in hand-to-hand combat training, and she was looking forward to this part the most.

Being in the CIA hadn't been what she'd pictured herself doing. She'd been a senior at MIT when a recruiter had approached her, and for some reason, when the job was offered, she hadn't hesitated. She'd said yes a year and a half ago, and she was incredibly close to completing the training she'd often thought of as endless.

Unlike the other computer whiz kids she had been working with, Brooke was athletic. She played volleyball and ran track throughout high school and college. She hadn't struggled with the early morning physical training programs that were required and enjoyed them far more than her fellow recruits.

She looked up from her breakfast and saw Patrick Bowing staring at her, something she caught him doing quite often. Had it been someone else, it probably would have bothered her. But Patrick was her best friend, teammate, and source of comic relief. She smiled, and his dark eyes lit up as they always did when Brooke acknowledged him. After a moment, he looked away, and she wondered, as she often did lately, if there was something he wasn't telling her. But as always, she pushed the thought aside, unwilling to deal with that kind of complication right now. If it came to a head, she'd deal with it then.

She shook off the thoughts and looked at the other three people sitting at her table. "Are you all looking forward to today?" There was no enthusiasm in the responses. If it was up to the majority of them, they'd stay inside all day perusing the ever-flowing river of knowledge from the systems they worked on. Hand-to-hand combat training wasn't even on their priority lists, let alone something they were looking forward to. Brooke had spent the last year watching her class dwindle from twenty to just the four of them seated at the table. They were the best at their jobs, and that had been proven time and time again. A new challenge was something that Brooke welcomed.

Jennifer Glass glanced up from underneath her rather lengthy dark bangs that she frequently swept to the side. "I heard our trainer is some hotshot Marine gunnery sergeant. Apparently, we're his first class, which is very bad news for all of us."

Brooke couldn't hold back her grin. "And why is that?"

Jennifer gave Brooke an obviously sarcastic glare as she leaned back in her seat. "Because not all of us are built the way you are, Hart." She rolled her eyes and returned to her food. Chris Carlson made up the last member of their remaining class, and he listened to Brooke and Jennifer exchange words without offering any input, which was his usual contribution. Brooke realized that there was no point in trying to boost their self-esteem or convince any of them that everything would be all right. The next six weeks would be difficult, and they all knew it. She picked up her tray. "See you all in there." She quickly walked past Patrick, squeezing his shoulder without saying a word.

❖

Tyler glanced through the profiles she had been given upon her arrival. *Jesus Christ, the CIA is thorough.* She realized that thought, in and of itself, was redundant. It was the frigging CIA. What else would they be? She would have four students for a six-week program. *Six measly weeks to teach these computer hacks combat training. Jesus, have budget cuts gotten that bad?* She pushed the folders aside and rested her head in her hands. What she needed to assess this group of people wouldn't be covered in any of the information she had been given. Instincts, a sense of surrounding, and the ability to deliver a fatal blow if required couldn't be ascertained by reading about where they grew up or their college transcripts.

She made her way to the small room adjacent to the classroom where they would be mustering. She briefly wondered if the CIA used the same lingo as the Marine Corps or if she should refer to mustering as roll call with her students. She shook her head. *Jitters. Just jitters. I've faced worse, right?* Tyler wanted to study their behavior when they entered the classroom, and like all classrooms at the Farm, she would be able to do so from here, on the other side of the two-way mirror.

maneuvers. Heavy bags, speed bags, and training dummies lined the large square, allowing adequate room for all. There was also an extensive weight training facility that would rival any professional sports team's equipment. The low hum of the air-conditioning unit was an always-present sound, which in Tyler's opinion was a poor replacement for the invigorating feeling of fresh air.

Tyler had changed into her standard-issue fatigue pants and a gray T-shirt that boasted USMC across the front. When the four recruits jogged up, she was impressed that they were all a few minutes early, and they immediately fell into their teams in a straight line facing her, awaiting further instruction. "We're going to start with the basics, straightforward bare-fisted fighting and takedown maneuvers. Besides being able to block an oncoming attack, you need to be able to counter and reevaluate for your next move. I need a volunteer…Hart, get up here."

Brooke closed the distance between them and took her fighting stance, sideways, facing Tyler.

Tyler had already ascertained that the training area was suitable for takedowns, as the ground was covered in matted flexible material, giving a little bounce when you walked. "I want you all to watch the following sequence, and then I'll take questions after." She looked at Brooke. "Okay, Hart, I just want you to do your best to block me. Act as if you're in a real-life situation. Treat me as a threat."

"Yes, ma'am."

Tyler came in slowly, wanting to gauge Brooke's abilities. Left punch, blocked; right hook, blocked; roundhouse kick, blocked. Tyler had already read her style, and as soon as Brooke blocked her second roundhouse, she used her other leg to sweep the feet out from under her. Tyler was on top of her

CHAPTER TWO

The first to enter the room was Brooke Hart. Tyler recognized her from her picture. She also remembered that this particular young woman was no stranger to a military way of life. Her father had been a career Naval officer, and because of this, Brooke had been raised on three different continents and spoke six languages. What Tyler wasn't expecting was her profoundly muscular frame. She was close to five foot seven, and it was clear she had spent years in extensive athletics. Although she was wearing standard-issue physical training clothes, her lean, firm muscles showed through. Tyler couldn't help but smile to herself. *Not your typical computer jockey.*

Brooke moved with an alluring combination of grace and confidence. Brooke leaned forward on her desk and took her seat, her exquisite forearms and triceps flexing. Tyler exhaled quickly. *Focus, Marine.*

The others filed in, and they were physically what Tyler had expected. The other three students were in decent shape, but she expected that was because their CIA training had required them to participate in PT every morning for the past year. She doubted it was something they'd do on their own. They spoke with each other casually, probably acutely aware of the two-way mirror that was to their right, as that kind of surveillance had been part of their lives for some time. Tyler glanced down at her beaten watch. Zero eight thirty. Time to get started.

Tyler opened the door and was a bit surprised when no one turned around. She thought to herself that perhaps they had far more military bearing then she was anticipating. The room simply fell silent as she walked to the front to face her students. The room could easily be mistaken for a small high school classroom, right down to the chairs with tabletops attached; a clean, shimmering whiteboard; and fluorescent lighting which, as usual, was particularly harsh. The typical off-white tiles kept everything uniform and without distraction. Her single desk sat in the front, facing those who would, in a few moments, become her students. When she reached the front of the room and the desk that would essentially be for decoration, she turned around and leaned against it with her hands gripping the sides of the fake wood.

She tried not to look as though she needed the support, the grounding, although she did. She'd never considered teaching as a career choice, and Tyler could tell as she examined their faces that they were taken off guard. *They were expecting a man.* She glanced over at Brooke Hart, who had turned a light shade of red but successfully hid whatever emotion she was feeling. The clear green eyes made Tyler's stomach flutter, and she swallowed to suppress the feeling. *Just more jitters. Relax.* Tyler pulled open the drawers to her desk in order to physically distract herself. There was a clipboard.

"I'm Gunnery Sergeant Tyler Monroe. I'll be your instructor for the next six weeks. Since I know you're all wondering, I am not officially CIA. I'm on loan from the Marine Corps. I am here to teach you how to defend yourself and kill if need be. I won't waste your time with a lengthy introduction. I would rather get right into it. Now, pair off into teams while I take muster—roll call." Quickly, the

recruits paired themselves off, and Tyler paced the fi the room, holding the muster sheet on the clipboard sl found. Somehow, it made her feel more official and ga something to do with her hands. She pointed to Brooke a man sitting next to her. "Names?"

"Brooke Hart and Patrick Bowing, ma'am." Br responded before Patrick had an opportunity.

Tyler glanced up from her clipboard and moved her toward the other two recruits. "And you two?"

"Jennifer Glass and Chris Carlson, ma'am."

Tyler was writing down the pairings as she walked ou the classroom. "If you need to use the head, do it. If you n to change, take care of it. I expect to see you all in the yard exactly ten minutes." Tyler walked out without looking up a was gone.

Jennifer gave out a long breath. "That was definitely n what I expected."

Brooke smiled at Patrick. "I don't know. I think this i going to be kind of fun."

Patrick grinned. "You would."

As Brooke walked out of the classroom she considered the blond sergeant with the serious, piercing blue eyes. *Yes, this could be lots of fun.*

❖

"The yard" was a training facility that still held on to its traditional name out of nostalgia, although the upgrades to the facility over the decades were apparent and included more inside than out. The outside portion included a full track and obstacle course, and the inside was made up of a sixty-foot-by-sixty-foot training area, complete with wall-to-wall mirrors, so that recruits were able to judge and improve all of their

in the blink of an eye, simulating placing a knife at Brooke's throat.

Tyler pushed herself up in one swift motion away from Brooke, and quickly glanced at her hands, hoping that they weren't shaking from the physical contact with the recruit. Tyler shook off the warm sensation that had flushed through her body. "Any questions before you start working on this with your teams?" No one raised a hand, although Tyler expected there was some confusion. "How about we just get started and I'll observe and help you along the way." As she moved between the pairs of students, she tried to push her errant thoughts away. No one had looked that deeply into her eyes in a very long time.

The group continued to perform that exercise, and a few other basic maneuvers, for the next several hours. She was impressed by how quickly they were picking it up, especially for four computer geeks. However, she was overly careful every time she passed Brooke, not wanting a repeat of the sensations provoked when she'd been on top of her.

Eventually, the two teams stood facing her, looking as if the last drop of their energy threatened to hit the floor. Tyler put her hands on her hips and regarded each of them. "Okay, that's enough for today. When we muster tomorrow morning, we're going to go through everything again quickly and then we'll move on. I need to know if you're having trouble keeping up, because these techniques could be the difference between life and death for you or someone else." She paused for another moment, letting her words sink in. "That's it. See you in the morning."

The recruits started filing out of the yard, and Tyler smiled to herself, knowing she was pushing their bodies further than any of them had ever thought possible. *Well, most of them, anyway.* She watched Brooke walk out with a little more bounce in her step than her peers. She placed her hand on Patrick's shoulder, a seemingly comforting gesture.

Tyler didn't mean to eavesdrop, but she couldn't help but overhear the recruits as they were walking away, one conversation in particular. Brooke was reassuring Patrick about his abilities. She was supportive, nurturing. Brooke had the makings of an effective leader and a team player. It wasn't often the two traits were present in a single person involved in military or intelligence agency work. Tyler was impressed. The recruits made plans to meet for dinner, and Tyler noticed the smile that Patrick beamed in Brooke's direction. It seemed affectionate, and his eyes read of devotion and admiration. The realization made Tyler a bit uneasy, and for the thousandth time that day, she tried to shake off the feelings that seemed to be associated with Brooke Hart.

She changed out of her fatigues and into running shorts with a ribbed black tank top. Working basic maneuvers all day wasn't quenching her need to exercise her muscles completely. As she walked back into the yard, she recognized the figure over in the corner, stretching. What wouldn't have typically given her pause made her stomach tighten and her palms grow clammy. She watched Brooke, legs shoulder width apart, stretch down to the ground, hands around her ankles.

Tyler's physical reaction wasn't because of the way she could see the perfectly formed muscles move and flex or even because of the small glimpse that she was able to gain of Brooke's back and the way her muscles twitched. It was because at that moment, Tyler didn't think that she had ever seen anything more beautiful in her life.

Tyler tried her best to focus on her workout and ignore the nagging desire to look over at Brooke. Before she had a moment to completely get her thoughts straight, Brooke had popped up and was jogging in Tyler's direction. Tyler studied Brooke's face once she was in front of her. She looked a little unsure of herself, as though searching for something to say.

Brooke broke the silence. "Do you need a spotter?"

Tyler looked up at Brooke as she was tightening her gloves. "Haven't had enough for one day, Hart?" Brooke's face went a little pale, and Tyler hid her smile.

"I just figured I would check before I hit the showers. We're told to never lift alone."

Tyler placed her hands on the bars and pushed up, considering Brooke's question. She didn't actually need a spotter, she was doing light weights, but the idea of having Brooke that close was an intriguing one. The thought alone frightened her. She was caught up in her own mental back-and-forth, weighing the appropriateness of inviting this recruit's closeness when she already knew how her body would react. She wasn't aware how much time she had let pass without an answer to a very simple question.

Tyler sat up to rest just as Brooke turned to leave. She should have let her go without saying anything, but before she could stop herself, she blurted out, "You did very well today, Hart. I was impressed."

Brooke stopped in her tracks but didn't turn around to face her. She barely whispered, "Thank you, ma'am."

Tyler watched Brooke walk away, unable to think of anything more to say.

❖

When Brooke arrived for dinner, her classmates were busy rehashing the day's events, but she was only half listening to their conversation. The mess hall, like most other rooms at the Farm, offered little viable distraction. Long tables with benches a dirty beige color, matching trays, and an overwhelming smell of cleaners mixed with creamed corn. The high windows afforded a glimpse of the ending day and brought a hint of coral shadow only a sunset could provide.

The other part of her mind, the part that seemed to dominate her thoughts at the moment, was remembering what Tyler looked like when she briefly had her body pinned to the ground. Brooke could still feel the sensations that washed over her in those brief moments. The warming sensation started in her chest and quickly moved through the rest of her body. Then the memory of those eyes came into focus, the steely blue Brooke could have spent hours, if not days, examining and memorizing. She only slightly registered that there were other people around her. When a morsel of bread hit her in the forehead, she looked up at Jennifer.

"What the hell is your problem, Hart?"

Brooke blankly looked at Jennifer, whose face still seemed to be flushed from the day's training. "Nothing, sorry. Guess I'm just tired."

Chris gave a small huff. "Tomorrow is going to be rough. I'm sore in places I didn't know I had."

Patrick chimed in without missing a beat. "It's just six weeks. We can do anything for six weeks." His statement came out as almost a question.

Jennifer looked around to see who else was in listening distance from their table before she leaned in and started speaking softly. "Well, I did some work of my own during our brief interlude."

Patrick and Chris looked at her, interested; Brooke shifted uneasily in her seat. She had gotten to know Jennifer over the last year, and one thing was for certain, she loved a little gossip.

"I was able to pull up the file on our dear Sergeant Monroe.

She's some sort of Marine Corps legend. Her service record is impeccable, and all her evaluations rave about her devotion to duty, her sense of patriotism, and her commitment to the mission." She moved a couple of pieces of food around on her plate. "Then, six months ago, there was an attack on her unit while they were moving in on a target. Every single member of her team was killed except her. She sustained some pretty serious injuries, and they shipped her over here."

Brooke bit her lip. *She must have been devastated.* She couldn't even begin to fathom what that would do to a person.

"Basically, our instructor is damaged goods," Jennifer added with a tone of finality.

Patrick, who was clearly taken aback by Jennifer's remark, said, "How can you say that? You have no idea what she has gone through, and I for one would rather have someone like her teaching me hand-to-hand combat than someone who's been behind a desk their whole life."

Jennifer gave a small grunt and spoke under her breath. "Not that it did her unit any good."

Brooke was about to defend Tyler and started to lean across the table to speak, when she felt Patrick's hand on her shoulder. He shook his head, letting her know it wasn't worth arguing.

The four of them finished the rest of their meal in almost complete silence until Chris said softly, "At least she's unbelievably hot."

Jennifer nodded. "Well now, that's an understatement."

Brooke felt her body tighten. She wasn't sure why, but she wasn't comfortable having her peers discuss how disarmingly attractive their new instructor was. After the meal was finished, they said their good nights and headed for their dorm-like rooms. It needed to be an early night, and they were going to need all the rest they could get. Brooke slid into bed with her book at her side, but she couldn't concentrate. When she turned out the light, dances of hand-to-hand combat became another kind of dance entirely, and though her opponent was in shadow, there wasn't really any question who it was. The cadence of Tyler's voice and her fluid gestures eased her into what would be a night of uneasy rest.

CHAPTER THREE

Thompson."
 Right after he pushed the talk button on his Bluetooth, Michael Thompson walked to the window of his office. From the forty-eighth floor, he could see almost all of downtown New York City. He found the constant movement below soothing. From this height, the chaos down below seemed organized, with a flow and a purpose. Organization and purpose, in Thompson's mind, were a necessity. The whiney female voice of the computer programmer that Lark had assigned didn't have Thompson's charisma or appeal, but she had resources and skills that meant he didn't have to get his own hands dirty. He pinched the bridge of his nose; the irritation he was feeling was just the tip of the iceberg. "I need you to get the program ready. You know the orders as well as I do. Just take care of it." He hung up before the complaining and questions became more than he could handle.

He looked at the clock on his desk and fought the urge to violently swipe everything onto the floor. He hated that so much of what he wanted and needed to accomplish hinged on the actions of another person. *One questionably intelligent person.* A single photograph on his desk seemed to glare back at him. A slightly younger version of himself stood next to his mother and his brother, who wore his newly pressed Marine Corps uniform. He felt the hatred and disgust start to boil in his belly once again. He practically growled as he grabbed his jacket and stormed out of his office.

❖

Tyler waited outside the director's office at zero-seven forty-five. The hallway reminded her of a hospital, with its white walls and sterile smell; the only thing missing was the generic landscape pictures that seemed to be standard in hospitals and cheap motel rooms. She glanced at the receptionist, who seemed overwhelmingly busy for a person whose day didn't officially start for another fifteen minutes.

She briefly looked up at Tyler after answering her phone. "He's ready for you. Go on in."

Tyler passed the stressed woman and made a mental note to bring coffee for her the next time she was summoned. *People do that for each other, right? Bring coffee?*

Mark Broadus was exactly what Tyler had expected— early fifties, salt-and-pepper hair, with a body that had slowly declined from fit to fat from long years at a desk. Tyler had spoken to Broadus on the phone prior to her arrival. He seemed excited to have her on board.

"Gunnery Sergeant," he said with a small smile on his face. "I take it that you've settled in and everything is going fine?"

Tyler didn't sit because he hadn't asked her to as of yet, and her military training didn't allow her to make such a determination on her own when talking to a superior officer. "Yes, sir, everything is fine, sir."

He motioned to the chair beside her, and when she sat, he

did as well. "I know that this isn't nearly as exciting as being in the deserts of Iraq, but training is essential to the mission, and we're thrilled to have you here."

Tyler sat with her palms flat against her legs, trying to ignore the slight sweat that began in her palms at the mention of Iraq. "I'm up for the challenge, sir."

Broadus flipped through some notes on a yellow legal pad. "I see right now you're working with our tech specialists." He briefly looked up at her, waiting for a nod. "Bright kids, all of them. Looks like they have a lot of potential. They've been whittled down from a group of more than twenty over the last year, and I would hate for any of them to wash out at this stage in the game. I hope that they're able to catch on to your regimen."

Tyler nodded. "They'll be fine, sir. I won't let them fail."

Broadus gave a small laugh. "I don't imagine that you would, Sergeant." He stood. "Thank you for coming in, and please feel free to stop by if there are any issues."

Tyler walked out of the office and shut the door. She was relieved the meeting hadn't been long or drawn out. Broadus seemed to have the same mentality of every military officer she had ever worked with, straight, to the point, and no fluff. He wanted her to respect him and vice versa. She was here to do a job and she was going to do it well.

❖

Brooke was running late, or what she perceived to be late, and cut through the building at a steady jog. She had overslept, which wasn't like her, but she'd been unable to banish the image of Tyler from her mind, and the thoughts had left her lonely and awake until almost zero five hundred.

Brooke yawned as she turned the corner and ran head on into Tyler. Coffee spilled down the front of Tyler's shirt, and tons of folders scattered across the neatly waxed hallway tiles.

"Shit." Brooke quickly tried to put the folders back together.

"Good morning, Hart." Tyler looked down at the front of her shirt, now covered in black caffeinated liquid.

"Sorry about that, ma'am. I didn't want to be late for class, and I didn't see you." Brooke could feel her face burning with embarrassment.

Tyler bent down and began helping gather the folders. "Well, it looks like we should start honing situational awareness skills in class."

Brooke glanced up to see Tyler giving a sly grin and realized she was trying to make light of the situation. The knot in her stomach loosened slightly. Brooke took the folders in her arms. "I'll put these in the classroom for you, so you can change."

Tyler looked at her watch. "I don't have enough time to go back to my quarters, but I have an extra shirt in my gym bag in the training room, so I'll just throw that on."

They walked down the hall and turned into the room without saying another word, but Brooke once again felt dizzy. She could swear there was an actual current between them. *What is it about this woman that makes me behave like a teenager whenever I'm anywhere near her?* Even slightly bumping against Tyler's arm before she turned into the room left her skin tingling and warm.

Brooke placed the files on the desk while Tyler picked up her gym bag from the desk and found a shirt. She looked away when Tyler turned her back and pulled off her shirt, placing it into her bag. But as Tyler was pulling the fresh shirt on, Brooke couldn't help but take a not-so-innocent look at her back. It was muscular and defined, the product of thousands of push-ups and combat training. She stifled a groan of disappointment when the new shirt was fully on and Tyler was tucking it into her pants. Brooke quickly turned back around and worried Tyler would see the desire she knew was painted across her face.

The rest of the class entered into the room, and the silence between Tyler and Brooke was almost palpable. Jennifer gave Brooke a questioning glance as she took her seat, looking between them.

Patrick was the last to enter the room. "I was waiting for you this morning."

He looked at Brooke, not with anger, but worry, and Brooke shook herself out of the moment. "Sorry, I was running late and came straight here."

Patrick frowned, clearly wanting to ask questions, but there was no time to discuss anything else.

Tyler had already started to move toward the door. "Since everyone is accounted for, get your butts out to the yard so we can get started."

❖

Glass had Carlson flat on his stomach, his hand wrenched and her knee square in his back. "Perfect," Tyler said as she moved past the pair. They had been at these maneuvers for hours, and Tyler was impressed with the class's progression. She hadn't expected them to be such quick studies. "We're going to be moving on to weapons before you know it." Tyler came to a standstill in front of the recruits. "We're going to put this into action now. I want everyone to make a circle and one person will start in the middle. One at a time, each of you will attack the person in the center, and when he or she gets taken down, you will replace them. Last person standing won't have to run the three miles we're going to complete at the end of class."

Jennifer Glass was the first to step into the middle. Tyler liked her. Sure, she could smell the attitude coming off her, and her arrogance could be grating at times, but those little character flaws were what made her interesting. Underneath it, Tyler really believed that she would make a fine soldier, even if that soldiering would only ever be done from behind a desk.

The group went at it for almost fifteen minutes. Tyler was more than impressed that it was taking so long for each person to be pushed out. She was only slightly disappointed that the sparring had yet to afford Brooke the opportunity to get involved, and when it was Brooke that finally knocked Patrick out of the center, Tyler felt an emotion that resembled pride though she had no idea why.

Brooke moved with absolute grace and agility. It was clear that athleticism was something that came naturally to her, as did combat training, apparently. She could see in Brooke's face that she could anticipate her opponent's next move and counter it as such. She knocked down each of her contenders within three moves of them entering to challenge her. Tyler would have been lying to herself if she didn't admit how much she liked seeing Brooke in this environment. *She's passionate. Focused. Like her life depends on it.* When Brooke had fended off the last of her peers, she stopped, put her hands on her hips, and smiled at Tyler. *I could get lost in that smile.* The thought snapped Tyler out of her daze and prevented her from smiling back.

"Good job, Hart. Okay, everyone, let's start our run. Hart, you can stay back and relax, enjoy the fruits of victory." The class started moving with a few moans and protests as they began their run.

"If it's all the same to you, ma'am, I would rather just run with the class."

Tyler nodded, glad Brooke would be joining them and trying desperately not to consider why. "That's fine, Hart."

❖

The class was just completing their run, and as usual, Tyler was impressed with Brooke. Carlson brought up the back end of the pack, and Brooke slowed down to run with him. When all four of them had completed their three-mile jaunt, they stood in a circle, drank water, and tried to catch their breath. Carlson grabbed Brooke's shoulder appreciatively. Tyler, who had barely broken a sweat, praised her class. "Good job, everyone. Tomorrow, we'll cover the maneuvers you learned for the last few days, and then we'll begin weapons training." The class started to head to the locker rooms, but Brooke hung back under the pretense of needing to tie her shoes, apparently very, very slowly.

Tyler tried to ignore the overwhelming sensation to walk over and talk to her, and just as she thought she had mustered the strength to walk away, she heard Brooke's voice.

"Ma'am, I hate to bother you, but I was hoping you could help me with a few of the techniques we've been covering."

Tyler turned and looked at Brooke. Her hands were on her hips, and a few stray hairs were in her eyes. Her shirt was damp with perspiration and her left dimple sent a jolt of arousal to the pit of Tyler's stomach. *Tell her no. Tell her you have to be at a meeting. Tell her she'd be better off practicing with one of her classmates.* "Sure thing, Hart. Happy to help." *You're an idiot, Monroe.*

They made their way over to the center of the room and took their stances. "If you want extra training, I'm going to go harder on you than we do in class. If it becomes too much, let me know and we'll re-cover the things we've learned so far." As Tyler said it, she knew that part of the reason she wanted to step it up a level with Brooke was so that she could focus on something other than wanting to put her mouth all over Brooke's body.

"Roger that, ma'am." Brooke grinned and made a "come on" gesture with her hands.

Tyler grinned back and nodded. The sparring started out slowly, with Tyler taking the defense as she allowed Brooke to practice her maneuvers. Tyler was mentally critiquing Brooke's form when she suddenly found Brooke's arm around her neck and her back pressed against Brooke's chest. The heavy breathing on her neck from the sparring and the press of Brooke's breasts against her back was almost her undoing. Brooke loosened her grip to get a better hold, and Tyler pushed her hand between her neck and Brooke's arm, spinning her around and reversing the position. With her mouth against Brooke's ear, she whispered, "Don't ever let up, even for a moment. Those moments are our greatest weaknesses." She pushed Brooke away, trying to gather herself without letting her see how rattled she was.

They stood facing each other with only a few feet between them, catching their breath. Tyler wanted nothing more than to put her hands all over Brooke's body, to feel the tight muscles she knew were pulsing under her shirt. She shook the thought away. "Let's take a water break." They grabbed their water bottles and sat on the floor.

After a few moments, Brooke looked at Tyler. "Can I ask you something?"

Tyler only nodded. Questions like that often opened doors

better not walked through, but she couldn't shut Brooke out so obviously.

"How long were you in the Marine Corps?"

Tyler shrugged, stretched her leg muscles, and tried to ignore her body's reaction to Brooke. "Ten years. I went in when I was eighteen."

Brooke stretched her legs as well. "So you're only three years older than me."

Tyler froze momentarily. She hadn't actually considered how close in age they were. Maybe, if they'd met somewhere else, some other time, things could have been different. She couldn't help but notice the smile that lingered on Brooke's mouth. *Perfect lips.* She should put a stop to the questions, to any more personal information. She was an instructor. Brooke was a recruit. Even being friends might be frowned upon. Not to mention that the three years in age difference didn't make up for utterly different experiences they'd had. Experiences that often made Tyler feel far older than she was.

Brooke finally broke the awkward silence. "Do you think we could go one more round...without you holding back?" She gave a Tyler a smile that left her no option but to get up and concede to her wishes. With fists up in the fighting position, they began again.

Tyler didn't hold back this time. In fact, she sparred with Brooke the same way she would with any man in her unit. Punching, blocking, kicking, they went on countering each other; offense, defense. Tyler was impressed by Brooke's natural inclination for hand-to-hand combat. She tried to lure Brooke in and make a final leg sweep, but was momentarily caught off guard by the combination of Brooke's scented soap, mixed with her sweat. It made her stomach lurch with excitement, and she found herself flat on her back, Brooke pinning her down. Tyler had only ever been pinned twice before, and both were during her early training days. She should have been disappointed with herself, angry at her obvious lack of attention to detail, but with Brooke's body so close to her own, her only awareness was that Brooke's leg was pressed very firmly between her own, locking her down.

Tyler let out a small wavering breath mixed with reluctance and rapidly growing arousal. Brooke lessened the grip on Tyler's wrists, and she pushed herself up on her elbows. Brooke moved closer and was about to press her mouth to Tyler's when the door swung open and Glass came walking through.

Snapped back to reality, Tyler flipped Brooke over and reversed the pin. She only held Brooke in the position for a passing second before she let her up. Glass seemed focused on a thick, daunting manual that she carried as she walked through the facility and didn't even glance in their direction. As Tyler wiped the sweat off her face, she turned her back to Brooke and started to walk away. "That's enough for today, Hart. I'll see you tomorrow." Tyler's equilibrium was still off as she grabbed her bag and walked out of the room.

❖

Tyler showered in an attempt to get her body under control, and once she felt somewhat normal again, she headed for the instructors' corridor. She needed to get her mind off Brooke, and being around other people might help. When she walked into the dining hall, she took stock of her fellow instructors. The people in the room made the large hall seem even bigger, as if it could sit well over a hundred people as opposed to the ten that were currently inside. Most of them were no doubt career CIA. They looked as she assumed they would, wearing suits or pressed dress pants and collared shirts. She made her way over to a table where a man and woman who looked relatively close to her age sat.

"You must be Gunnery Sergeant Monroe," the good-looking dark-haired man said. "We heard you were around here somewhere. It's always news when a new face shows up."

His eyes were almost the color of midnight and clear, and the only visual facial hair was the slight darkening around his mouth, showing that he had been up very early in the morning to shave. His posture and voice were friendly and inviting, and Tyler felt more at ease.

"I am." Tyler smiled back. It had been a long time since she'd been at ease enough to sit and talk to other people. *Maybe the shrink is right. Maybe it will get easier.*

"I'm Kyle King." He held out his hand. When she took it, he nodded at the woman. "That's Nicole Sable. We're part of the anti-terrorism training division."

The blond woman gave Tyler a genuine smile. "Welcome."

"I'm happy to be here." Tyler was surprised she actually meant it.

Nicole leaned over the table and said softly, "Kyle and I are going to head out to one of the local bars tonight. You should join us. Take a break for a while. Let us show you around some."

Tyler wanted to say yes but hesitated because she knew she had a class in the morning. "I would love to, but I have an early day tomorrow."

Kyle waved away Tyler's objection. "Tomorrow is Saturday. Classes don't start until ten hundred, and all the recruits have testing from oh eight hundred until ten hundred. You'll be fine."

Tyler couldn't think of a reason not to go. *Hell, maybe it will get my mind off Brooke.* "Okay, great. Should I meet you there?"

Nicole got up. "Nah, we'll make Kyle drive. Meet us out in front at twenty-one hundred." As she turned to leave she gave Kyle a small wink and walked away from the table.

Tyler noticed Kyle giving Nicole an appreciative full-body once-over. As she was getting up to leave, she chuckled in Kyle's direction. "See you both tonight, and thanks for the invite."

Kyle pulled himself away from watching Nicole's body sway back and forth. "No problem."

Instructors weren't required to live at Camp Peary. Tyler chose to do so because she didn't see the sense in establishing a residence at a duty station she wasn't going to remain. When she was getting ready to go out later, she wondered if Kyle and Nicole stayed on site. *I seriously doubt it. This place doesn't exactly scream independence and good times.* As she searched through the few articles of clothing she had with her, she wondered what Brooke would look like if she were going out for the evening. *Fantastic, Monroe, keep fantasizing. That's helpful.* Tyler decided on a pair of faded blue jeans, a fitted black T-shirt, a gray blazer, and black boots. She looked at herself in the full-length mirror behind her door. *This is as good as it is going to get.* Rationally, Tyler knew her body was healed. She wasn't missing a limb, there weren't any scars that couldn't be covered, but she still felt as if parts of her were missing.

She'd felt her shin snap. Or, as her doctor had informed her later, her tibia. The pain was immediate and throbbing; the wound was bloody and jagged. The protruding bone was an indicator in and of itself, but she didn't feel it to the full extent until she was in transit to the hospital. *The only one in transit.* When the doctor had first explained her injury, his words were hazy, blurry. The images of everything she had left on the roadside were still swirling in her head. Her seemingly minor injury didn't seem of much importance. It was aggravating to hear mumblings of four to six months with physical therapy. The doctor went on to tell her how lucky she was that this was her only real injury. The minor burns would heal, possibly without scarring. The cuts, bruises, they would all go away. The word that stuck with her, that he had thrown out so easily, as if he were trying to comfort her, felt more like another piece of shrapnel lodged in her heart: lucky. She didn't feel lucky. She felt responsible.

Responsible. She hadn't been able to identify that nagging, unforgiving emotion for a long time. But when the Marine Corps tells you you're going to therapy twice a week until they're convinced you're better, you go. The realization was supposed to make her feel better. Being able to pinpoint what she was feeling and talk about it was supposed to help. All it did was cement her realization that although it wasn't technically her fault, she was responsible for every one of those lives. She was their leader, they trusted her, and she couldn't save them.

It hadn't taken the full six months for her shin to recover, only a little over four. The doctors and physical therapists praised her for her progress almost daily. She never dared to tell them that she enjoyed the pain. Pushing through the agony, the sweat, and the tears was her penance. Part of her hoped it would never end. But it did. It did and then her next assignment came, technically a desk assignment, at Camp Peary.

The reflection in the mirror was whole, but Tyler wasn't. Images of her team, her friends, came flooding back. The people she was closest to, people she had shared drinks and laughs with, people she would sit with at night and talk about their lives back home and who was waiting for them when they returned. And then…their bodies lying lifeless in the unforgiving Iraqi sand. She felt the loss and pain start to rise in the back of her throat. She pushed it down and closed her eyes, taking deep breaths, just as her psychiatrist had advised. She managed to regain control of her senses after only a few minutes. She only allowed herself another half glance in the mirror, not long enough to let the memories return again.

❖

Brooke had known she should move, that she should get off Tyler immediately. She didn't understand what had held her there, why she couldn't bring herself to look away from the deep blue eyes that were rapidly getting even darker. She had felt Tyler's tight, firm muscles under her own body twitch, and instead of registering that it was her instructor pinned underneath her, she could only think about how much she wanted her to keep twitching. She had wanted to pull her shirt off and run her mouth all over her taut stomach, exploring every inch of her.

Tyler had looked as if she was in pain, not physical pain, but stinging with the pain of desire. Brooke might have only been with a few women, but she drew enough attention to know what yearning looked like. The thought of Tyler wanting her too only excited her more, and she had pressed her leg more firmly between Tyler's. She had wanted Tyler's response, and the fact they were in an open area hadn't occurred to her at all.

Brooke had watched Tyler walk out of the yard. Her body had continued to hum with need and confusion in equal measures. She couldn't remember a time when she had been so drawn to a woman, and it wasn't just because Tyler was beautiful. She had an aura about her. Strength, power, stability, and courage radiated off Tyler's body, and all Brooke knew was that she wanted to be closer; she wanted more.

After taking a lukewarm shower, Brooke headed for the other side of the facility to use one of the pay phones. The recruits were allowed to have cell phones during their training, but Brooke opted not to. She liked being able to contact her family when she felt the need, not the other way around. She picked up the receiver, pulled the phone card out of her pocket, and dialed the familiar number sequence, though she secretly hoped no one was there to answer her call.

She hadn't had a bad childhood, and her relationship with her parents was fine. But Brooke felt like a bit of an outsider when it came to her family, and it often felt like they agreed with that sentiment. She was the youngest of three children and the only girl. Her father had doted on her most of her life, and her mother never missed an opportunity to tell Brooke how beautiful she was. However, she also believed that Brooke was making a mistake going to work for the government, although she really wasn't aware of the full scope of Brooke's job. She just preferred her to be in an office building somewhere, wearing designer dresses and perusing the city for a successful husband. None of those things had ever held any interest for Brooke.

Her parents knew Brooke was gay. She had come out to them her junior year in high school when she had fallen head over heels for the setter on her volleyball team. They just chose to ignore this aspect of her life, still shrugging it off as a phase. Brooke had to admit, she made it easy for them to do so. Her first romance had fizzled out as high school drew to a close when Veronica had been awarded a volleyball scholarship to UCLA, essentially ending their relationship before it progressed beyond adolescent adoration.

Since high school, Brooke had had a select few encounters with women, none of them ever amounting to much. She had never met anyone that warranted dating past four months or taking home to meet her parents. Brooke needed to be stimulated emotionally, physically, and mentally, and she had yet to find anyone that fulfilled all three, but she was willing to wait rather than settle.

Her brothers were both career military, and Brooke often wondered why her mother felt it was good enough for them but not for her. *Ridiculous double standards.* One ring, two rings, three rings. *I may have gotten lucky.*

"Hello?" Her mom sounded like she was in a good mood, and Brooke assumed it was because it was nearly seventeen hundred, and her mom was on her second glass of merlot.

"Hi, Mom, how are you?" Her mother went on for nearly six minutes about her weekly activities, something she subjected Brooke to every time she called. She even went into detail regarding her father's golf game and how it had greatly improved since his retirement. Brooke was thankful that her mother couldn't see her face, as she was consistently rolling her eyes.

"Are you almost done with this never-ending training?" She sounded hopeful and excited. Brooke wasn't sure if that was because she wanted her home or if she was actually coming around to her chosen line of work.

"Actually, just a few more weeks and I'm all finished up."

"Oh." She sounded a little surprised. "Then we should be expecting a visit shortly after. I'll let everyone know. Maybe your brothers can make it."

Brooke was trying to find the right spot to interrupt her, and one finally came when her mom got distracted by the dog moving around at her feet. "No, Mom, I don't know where I'll be after this. I'll let you know as soon as I do, though."

Her mother gave out a long sigh. "I don't like this, Brookie. Never knowing exactly where you are or when you'll be coming home. It's not right."

The irony didn't escape Brooke that her mom had spent

over thirty years never really knowing the whereabouts of her husband, and now her sons. "Okay, Mom. I love you. Say hi to Dad for me." Brooke could tell her mom wasn't ready to get off the phone yet, but allowed her to end the call anyway.

"Okay, sweetheart, talk to you soon."

Conversations with her mother were never soothing, and Brooke was always glad when they were over. She knew her mom meant well. She knew her parents loved her and wanted what was best for her. Brooke just wished that what they wanted for her and what she wanted for herself were in alignment. Until she could settle the two, she didn't believe she could have the type of relationship she really wanted with her parents, a relationship that was open, honest, and had mutual respect. She was walking back to her side of the complex on near autopilot, making a mental checklist of things she needed to study for her exam in the morning, when she saw Tyler gliding down the steps toward the front gate.

The strategically placed lights that lined the sidewalks made it almost look like she was glowing. She was dressed casually and was still the most alluring woman Brooke had ever seen. Brooke moved behind a pillar so she could see but not be seen. *It's not spying. Just curiosity.*

Tyler's blond hair bounced on her shoulders as she made her way down the steps. Her clothes fit perfectly in all the right places, clinging to her solid frame, teasing at what she might look like without them. Brooke's throat went dry and her heart raced. Even in the darkness and from twenty feet away, she knew Tyler's eyes were still agonizingly beautiful. Brooke had an overwhelming desire to follow her, to see where she was going and with whom. A car pulled up, and a woman got out of the front seat and pushed the chair forward for Tyler to climb in the backseat.

Brooke couldn't get a clear view of the passenger's face and was mad at herself for not getting in a better position when she had the chance. *What's the matter with you? You're acting like a jealous girlfriend.* Brooke tried to shake off the feeling as she headed back to her room. *Come on, girl. You've worked too hard to get distracted now.*

CHAPTER FOUR

Thompson walked to the large windowpane in his twenty-eighth-floor penthouse apartment that overlooked downtown Manhattan. He grabbed a bottle of the twenty-year-old scotch that sat on his bar near the fireplace and poured himself a generous portion, ignoring the woman gathering her belongings behind him. Wearing only his boxers, he continued to stare out the window. "The money is on the counter." He would never admit to using a *hooker*; he simply considered it a business transaction with someone of the opposite sex. He had no desire to intertwine himself in personal relationships and found this was much less complicated, and cheaper, than trying to keep a girlfriend entertained. The woman was tall, thin, and glaringly beautiful. Her nightly rate was $10,000, and Thompson had left her an extra $5,000 so she'd remain on call for him whenever he beckoned. She didn't bother saying good-bye before she left. This was her sixth time with Thompson, and she was well aware he didn't want to participate in any conversation after their transaction.

Once she was gone, Thompson opened the top drawer of his desk and turned the small cell phone on. He had purchased the burner cell when he had originally started on this journey to infiltrate the CIA computer system. When he'd discovered that Tyler Monroe had been recently assigned to the facility, it had given him the push he needed to move forward with his plans. The text message icon lit up, and Thompson couldn't help but smile when he read the message from his insider at the Farm. "*Done.*" He closed the phone and dropped it into a glass of water. By the end of the day, he would have the USB drive back in his possession and could pass it on. *Today is going to be a good day.*

The courier arrived a little before four p.m. with a small gift basket. It was a nice display of wines and cheeses, something he often got when he closed a deal with a new client. He took the wedge of brie out, stuck his pocket knife inside, and pulled out a thumb drive wrapped in plastic. He was usually impressed with his abilities, and this instance was no different. The private courier would pick up the drive and deliver it to Mr. Lark. There would be no stopping their forward progress. As he took a small cracker out of the basket and spread the cheese across it, he loaded the sports message site where he and Lark exchanged messages. He opened a screen for the new post and read the message. *First round of playoffs will go to the underdogs, and I predict the score to be 07-45.* He closed the screen and enjoyed another cracker with cheese. Tomorrow, at seven forty-five a.m., the exchange would happen.

Thompson sent a message to Lark, then opened the encryption software plugged into his external hard drive, waiting for the systems to link. He had been able to obtain almost everything requested, although the parts he was missing were the ones his employer really wanted. The banks of computers kept in a vault inside the Farm resembled a similar setup in a room in Langley, Virginia, at CIA headquarters. They contained the most sought after identities in the entire world, not only CIA personnel but the identities and personal information of every covert officer that the United States was aware existed. The data included pictures, family information, aliases, and a plethora of other information that made people in Thompson's profession salivate.

The information was priceless and almost impossible to obtain. The fact that these vaults existed wasn't well known, and the location of the vaults was known by only two people, the director of Camp Peary and the director of the CIA. The information wasn't accessible from a network and could only be obtained by either of the directors after a series of ever-changing codes and passwords. It was, by far, the most difficult and exciting project Thompson had ever taken on.

However, what he really wanted was the opportunity to take down Tyler Monroe, the cowardly dyke bitch that had brought disciplinary action against his brother before getting him killed. The rumors of his brother's attempted rape had almost destroyed their mother, leaving her in a deep depression from which Thompson was sure she would never recover. Monroe was the reason his brother had been out with the rest of them on mission that day. The plan had always been for him to stay back, to be alone. Thompson didn't know the details of how she had forced him to go, but he knew it was her fault his brother had gone on the mission he didn't return from. He cringed at the thought of her ordering his brother around, thinking that she was superior like most women in today's world, with their ridiculous illusions of equality. He blew out the hatred like it was smoke, attempting to calm himself and regain focus.

He began to type, regurgitating the details of the mission he had obtained from his CIA informant. "Entry into facility will not be easy. There is one underground tunnel. Heavily guarded and reinforced by six-foot-thick steel plates, along with an electromagnetic field that will not permit transmissions of any kind. We will need twelve men to infiltrate and carry out the objective. Will make necessary arrangements from here and finalize all other plans at the rendezvous point in four weeks, twenty-two hundred." He read it once more before hovering the arrow over the send button while he did a final check. He clicked the mouse and watched the message dissolve into encryption, disappearing off the screen. Thompson grabbed his scotch off the table and walked back over to the window. *You're going to pay, bitch.*

❖

The bar was like most hole-in-the-wall establishments. Neon signs with a variety of beer and liquor names lined the walls. There was a pool table in the corner that had apparently beckoned to a group of men and women, who were watching the seemingly competitive game taking place. There were a few people shooting darts in the corner, and the jukebox played a classic rock song by the Doors as Tyler, Nicole, and Kyle walked over to an empty booth and took a seat.

Kyle placed his hand on Nicole's back. "First round is on me. What can I get you, Tyler?"

Tyler pushed the peanut shells that covered the table onto the floor. Though she wouldn't normally approve of such an action, the floor showed that was exactly where they belonged. "A beer is fine."

Kyle walked away, disappearing into a group of people near the bar.

Nicole moved along to the music with a warm smile on her face. "So tell me what you really think of your new job."

Tyler wasn't sure why, but she felt comfortable with Nicole and Kyle already. "It's different from what I'm used to, but I'm enjoying the change of pace. At least for now, it beats riding a desk in Washington waiting for my full medical release." Trying to change the subject, not wanting to discuss what had caused her medical issue in the first place, Tyler blurted out, "How long have you and Kyle been together?"

Nicole leaned back in the booth. "What makes you think we are?"

Tyler realized she might have crossed a line. She wasn't really familiar with the protocol at her new duty station. "I'm sorry. I didn't mean to overstep. I just assumed."

Nicole laughed and leaned forward to touch Tyler's arm. "Don't worry. I was just giving you a hard time. We're very much together." Nicole searched the room, and when she caught sight of Kyle, she smiled. "We met at this bar, actually, not long after I had been transferred to Camp Peary. We had seen each other at the complex, but neither of us had the nerve to talk to the other until we were here one night and he had indulged in one too many shots of tequila."

Kyle sauntered back up to the booth and placed the drinks on the table. "What did I miss?"

Nicole kissed his cheek. "Oh, I was just telling Tyler how you fell in love with me the first time we talked and how now you can't live without me." Kyle turned red and shook his head, clearly a little embarrassed but not refuting Nicole's statement.

The night continued, and they talked about where they grew up, their families, and their call to service. A few hours and several beers later, Kyle and Nicole walked hand in hand to the dance floor. Tyler sipped her beer and watched. They seemed so focused on each other, lost in each other's touch and gaze. For the first time since Tyler could remember, she longed for that connection. It was a lonely feeling she wasn't used to. She had always felt fulfilled by her unit, her mission, her drive, but here in this moment, her thoughts turned to

Brooke, and she wondered if she could ever have, or even deserved, something more. Tyler absently looked around the room, mostly lost in thought, when she noticed an attractive redhead looking at her.

After a few moments of eye contact, the woman made the trip across the bar and into the booth, taking a seat next to Tyler. She gave Tyler a lazy smile. "I haven't seen you here before."

Tyler's eyes widened, and she suppressed a laugh before the woman started again. "Ugh! Sounds like a terrible pickup line. I'm sorry."

Tyler shook her head, still smiling. "No, it's all right. I am new here."

The redhead pretended to think for a moment, strumming her fingers on the side of her face. "Let me guess. Camp Peary?"

Tyler nodded. "Now what on earth would make you think that?"

The woman's eyes seemed to sparkle, and she pushed a piece of hair behind her ear. "I was guessing, but now I know for sure. You didn't answer one way or the other, and that is very Camp Peary of you."

Tyler glanced at her friends, who were still moving together on the dance floor. Part of her wished they'd come back and save her from...herself? "I guess you caught me then. Maybe you should see if they're hiring. Your deduction skills are quite impressive."

A mischievous smile broke across the woman's face. "That isn't my only skill." She winked.

Tyler leaned in a little closer, not wanting to embarrass the woman. "I'm sure it's not. And please, don't take this the wrong way, because you're beautiful. I'm just here with friends tonight. I'm not looking for anything else."

The woman squeezed Tyler's leg. "If you change your mind, you know where to find me." She kissed Tyler on the cheek and walked back across the bar. Tyler shook her head. The woman was gorgeous, and she'd just sent her packing. She needed another psych eval.

Kyle and Nicole walked back to the booth a few moments later. Kyle motioned toward the woman who had just left. "You're quite the heartbreaker, aren't you, Monroe."

Tyler flushed and shrugged. "I don't know what that was."

Nicole pushed Tyler's shoulder. "Looks to me like you're starting to make friends." She finished the sentence with an approving chuckle.

Tyler smiled in agreement, although she was still a bit off-kilter. There was no logical reason for her to have dismissed the woman. She was beautiful, friendly, and seemed interested in short-lived fun. But Tyler couldn't force the image of Brooke out of her head throughout the conversation, and that alone was troublesome, especially because one of her intentions for the evening was to banish Brooke from her mind. Luckily, neither Nicole nor Kyle registered that there was anything off about Tyler's current thought process.

Kyle looked at his watch. "Come on, Casanova. Let's get back before you break any other hearts and we aren't welcome here anymore."

❖

Back at the Farm, Tyler said good night to Kyle and Nicole and decided to take a short walk around the complex. She wasn't ready to go to bed yet, and she did her best thinking while in silent motion.

After a few minutes, she found herself standing in front of the yard. She wasn't in the right clothes for a workout, but figured she'd go grab workout gear and come back. She loved working out when it was empty. As she passed the front door, she could hear someone hitting the heavy bag. She glanced down at her watch. 0015. Tyler decided to pop her head in and remind whoever was in there that they had testing in less than eight hours.

She slid her card through the security reader and pushed the bulky door open, and the beep signaled her admittance. *Shit.* Brooke Hart stood ten feet away, wearing neon blue shorts and a matching sports bra. Her body was glistening under the fluorescent lighting, and her skin was slightly red from what looked like an incredibly intense workout. *Walk out the door and don't come back. Walk out the door and don't come back.* Tyler turned around and placed her hand on the long bar to push the door open.

"Sergeant Monroe?"

Shit. "Sorry about that, Hart. See you in the morning."

"Well, wait. I'll walk back with you."

Shit. "Okay, yeah, that would be great." *No, it won't. Who are you kidding?* "I'll just wait out front for you." *Because you're a total idiot.* Apparently, all rational process was out the door when it came to her interactions with this woman.

Tyler stood out in front of the building waiting for Brooke with her faced tilted to the sky and her eyes closed. When she was in the Iraqi desert, she used to wait for moments like this, although they rarely happened, when the world was silent and everything seemed almost normal. Some nights she could almost convince herself that she was back home in North Carolina, lying in the grass looking at the stars with her best friend, Michelle. But when she opened her eyes, the truth would be there—a sky that always seemed to have a red lining from the oil fires constantly burning, the taste of sand, and the smell of dried blood forever in the back of her throat. Even here, in this moment, she couldn't tell if the silence brought her the comfort of familiarity or made her stomach turn.

"Sorry that took so long. I rinsed off real quick."

Brooke had almost jumped down the steps, landing only a few inches in front of Tyler. Her beautiful olive green eyes were soothing, and Tyler absently wondered when she'd last felt truly calm. "It's not a problem. Just enjoying the night air."

She gave her a small smile and started to walk. "I'm sure you don't get a lot of moments to enjoy the night air in Iraq."

Tyler was silent for several seconds. "No, you don't." Her answer wasn't confrontational or condescending; she stated it as a fact, which it was. She asked about Brooke's family, although she had the information in Brooke's file. The personal stuff, the moments, weren't in there though, and that's what she wanted to hear about.

"My parents are good people." Brooke stepped over a crack in the sidewalk, then another. "They're somewhat narrow-minded and can be a little overbearing, but they're good people."

Tyler listened intently, captivated by Brooke's voice. "They must be very proud of you."

Brooke raised one shoulder and half looked at Tyler. "No matter how many trophies I won, how impressive my grades were, or how well I behaved, I would never be one of them."

"One of who?" Tyler asked, a little taken aback by the sadness in Brooke's tone. How could any parent not be screaming their praise from the rooftops?

"One of my brothers." Brooke shrugged again. "I was the baby, the only girl. They all treated me like a fragile little flower, when all I really wanted was their acceptance. My parents still think that my sexuality is a phase, and I came out in high school. My mother was actually disappointed when I got into MIT, because it would be too strenuous and I wouldn't have enough time to devote to finding a husband."

Tyler subconsciously put her hand on Brooke's back as they continued to walk, not analyzing why she felt she needed to calm Brooke, to reassure her. "I've only known you for a week." Tyler shook her head. She couldn't find the words she wanted. *God, I'm terrible at this.* "I don't have any fancy way to put my thoughts into poetic words."

"What?" Brooke asked.

"I think you're amazing, Brooke. You're focused and driven, unbelievably smart, compassionate, truly fearless, and—" Tyler stopped for a moment, her heart pounding, and she could swear that there was a ringing in her ears. "Absolutely beautiful." The last part was said almost under her breath, and she wished the words hadn't made it out of her mouth.

They continued to walk silently, and Tyler wondered if she'd crossed the line and said something wrong after all. When they got closer to Tyler's building, Brooke put her hand on Tyler's arm and motioned for her to sit on the curb with her. Tyler hesitated for a moment and surveyed their surroundings. There wasn't anyone around, but Tyler knew there were cameras everywhere, even though they weren't noticeable. She also knew they'd already been pushing their luck on this walk. "Why don't you come up to my room for a minute and I'll make us some coffee?" Tyler asked.

Brooke tilted her head, smiling. "Looking to break a few rules tonight, Gunnery Sergeant?"

Tyler smiled. "It'll be fine. I'll keep my door open to stifle any rumors."

They headed for Tyler's room in silence. "If you aren't comfortable with this, you don't have to come in." Tyler didn't want Brooke to feel pressured.

"No, I want to," Brooke answered without hesitation.

Tyler's room held only the bare essentials, so she wasn't worried about it being presentable for company. Her few toiletries were on a small table near the dresser. There were no doors on the closet that held several uniforms and a few items of personal clothing, all of which were arranged by color. Tyler started the process of making coffee in her little four-cup pot and watched Brooke pick up the picture frames and study the images of the only four photos in the room. It was strange, watching someone look at something so private, but for some reason, she didn't really mind.

"That's my unit. We took that picture a day before our last mission."

A caring smile crossed Brooke's face. "You all look so happy, especially in the middle of a war. Is that normal?"

Tyler leaned back against the table and crossed her arms. "You become like family."

Brooke motioned at another photo, of a small child with a young woman. "Is this you?" Brooke asked, still examining the photo.

"Yes, that's my mother and me…I don't have any siblings. My parents were killed in a car accident when I was five."

Brooke looked at Tyler with unmistakable sympathy in her eyes. "I'm so sorry."

Tyler shook her head. "It was a long time ago. You have nothing to be sorry for. My aunt Claire and uncle Adam raised me." She pointed to the final picture frame. "They're incredible people." The picture was of Tyler in her full Marine Corps dress blues, with a woman in her mid-forties. "I was lucky I didn't have to go into the system like so many others. I never felt like I missed out on anything."

Brooke looked like she was waiting for more, so Tyler continued. "They worked really hard to give me everything

I could possibly want. I had planned on going into the Naval Academy to eventually become a JAG, a military lawyer, and I was on track to do just that."

Brooke looked up from the picture. "What happened to change your mind?"

Tyler sighed and felt the pain of an old memory. "Nine eleven happened. I was sixteen and my uncle was on a business trip in New York. The meeting was in the North Tower." Tears started to fill her eyes, and she blinked furiously to keep them from falling. "I wanted to be able to protect us from something like that ever happening again."

The room was silent. Tyler wished for noise, anything that would mask the sound of her memories that were about to spill down her cheeks in the form of tears. She had opened up to Brooke, something she wasn't accustomed to doing, and the part that scared her the most was that she was glad she had. Tyler felt relief, a momentary break from the guilt that had become part of her daily existence.

Brooke finally spoke. "I don't think I've ever known anyone like you, Tyler. Everything you've experienced should have shoved you down a tunnel of despair and self-loathing, but you're anything but that."

Tyler shook her head. "That's not true. I have more regrets than you can imagine. More things that I wish I could change than I'm capable of explaining."

Brooke moved closer, and Tyler watched it happen, powerless to tell her to stop. She watched her hand reach out and land on her arm. She watched it gently move down to her hand. She watched their fingers intertwine. The feeling of calm once again flushed through her body.

"That may be how you feel, Tyler, but that's not what I see."

Her mind screamed that this wasn't a situation she should

be in, not here in this room, in this complex, and with a recruit. She couldn't stop herself. Brooke's eyes held so much love, so much caring, and what seemed like an understanding of Tyler that she couldn't quite put her finger on. In that same moment, Tyler became acutely aware that their breathing had slightly increased and the rise and fall of Brooke's chest made her stomach clench. Brooke's eyes dropped from Tyler's gaze and moved down to her lips. Tyler took a step forward and cupped the back of Brooke's neck. She was instantly aware of the tingling radiating through her body just because of the simple gesture, and arousal swept over her faster than anything she had ever experienced.

Slowly, Brooke moved closer, placing her forehead against Tyler's, their lips inches apart, and Tyler could feel the increasing heat coming off Brooke's body, a heat that made her own body throb. Brooke took her free hand and touched Tyler's cheek. Tyler moved into the caress and bit down on her bottom lip. She watched Brooke's expression as she pressed their bodies together. Brooke's eyes seemed to get a bit hazy, and Tyler momentarily reveled in the effect she had on her. Then it happened. Brooke kissed her.

Tyler resisted at first, a plethora of warning thoughts going through her mind, but the jolt that spread like wildfire through her body banished those within seconds. She was certain she could actually hear her body humming and was worried that Brooke might be able to hear it too.

Brooke carefully moved her tongue into Tyler's mouth. It seemed almost cautious after her initial advance. Tyler briefly thought that she liked the impulsiveness in Brooke. As soon as she felt Brooke's mouth widening, Tyler deepened the kiss, pushing further into her. Brooke's arms went around Tyler's neck and pulled her even closer. Tyler did her best to suppress the groans that she was sure were coming from the back of her throat, but they only seemed to encourage Brooke. Tyler found the bottom of Brooke's shirt and slid her hands up her bare back, leaving goose bumps in her wake. When Tyler's hands grazed the outside of Brooke's breast, she gave out a small whimper, leaving Tyler's mind spinning.

Tyler broke the kiss and lifted Brooke onto the table. As soon as she sat, Brooke pulled Tyler back to her body. Brooke wrapped her legs round Tyler and began to kiss her neck. Tyler bit the bottom of Brooke's ear and felt her body shiver at her fingertips.

"I want you so incredibly bad," Brooke murmured while biting at Tyler's neck.

The broken breath obliterated any strength Tyler had left. She pulled off her jacket and shirt, and Brooke's eyes raked over her. Tyler was certain no other woman had ever made her wet with just a look.

"You're so incredibly beautiful." Brooke started to kiss Tyler's perfectly flat abdomen while tugging her belt lose.

The phone had rung three times before it registered with Tyler that the noise was coming from inside the room. The realization of what was happening almost physically slammed Tyler back into reality. She noticed the open door, allowing anyone who happened to be walking by to see what was taking place. She looked down at her shaking hands and willed them to stop.

She answered the phone. "Monroe." She was too late. The caller ID said BLOCKED. She placed the phone on the nightstand and turned around to look at Brooke, part of her hoping that this was all some strange dream and the other part of her hoping that it had really happened.

"I'm really sorry about that," Tyler said while pulling her shirt back on and looking at the ground, afraid to make eye contact. "You're a recruit here and I shouldn't have taken advantage of you like that."

Brooke crossed her arms over her chest. "You didn't take advantage of me, and I kissed you. Stop acting like you just committed a crime."

Her voice was starting to escalate, and Tyler could tell it was anger seeping through. "We did do something wrong. This isn't appropriate and it shouldn't have happened." She paused to gather the words she didn't want to say. "And it will never happen again."

Brooke's hands were gripping the table so tightly it looked like she might pull it apart. "We're both adults. No one is going to be hauled off to jail."

Tyler locked gazes with Brooke, determined to get her to understand. "Just because we can't be thrown in jail for something doesn't make it right. You could be kicked out of the program, and I could be transferred, or even worse, discharged."

Brooke shook her head. "Things aren't always black and white. Sometimes there is a gray area."

Tyler waved away the argument, signaling the conversation had come to an end. "Not in my world."

Brooke hopped off the table and moved toward the door, but seemed to change her mind and stopped in front of Tyler, her eyes flashing with anger.

Tyler stiffened under the scrutiny and looked into Brooke's eyes. Her desire for her hadn't diminished since the interruption, and Brooke's anger made her even sexier, if that was possible.

Brooke didn't break eye contact. "Is it really protocol that you're worried about? Or is it something else?"

Tyler shifted, uneasy with the question. She searched

inwardly, and flashes of pain and loss played like a kaleidoscope in her mind. There were so many pieces of Tyler's heart shattered into small shards from blow after blow over the years. She couldn't place those fragments at someone's feet. No one deserved that job, especially someone like Brooke. At Tyler's silence, a pain and anger flashed like lightning through Brooke's eyes, and she walked out without another word.

The part of Tyler she wasn't familiar with, the irrational part, wanted to go after Brooke, to grab her and tell her the effect that she had on her. She didn't go because her feet felt attached to the dull, lusterless flooring, like they had been planted there. She was overwhelmed with a paralyzing sense of loss. She had never felt the sudden absence of another woman like this before. She'd been with women, though they were usually no more than someone to warm her bed and scratch an itch. But even the ones that stirred emotions in Tyler never had an effect on her the way Brooke had in a week. Brooke not only blurred the lines of right and wrong that Tyler had used as a safety net for the last ten years, she made Tyler open up in ways she hadn't in years. But she knew that vulnerability equated to pain. Her heart couldn't take another break, especially at the hands of someone special like Brooke. She pulled off her clothes and lay down, knowing sleep was a long way off.

Talking about her uncle Adam with Brooke had stirred emotions in Tyler that she hadn't examined in a very long time. The day that changed her and her aunt's lives forever wasn't one she would ever forget. Tyler had already been at school for two hours, participating in ROTC, when the news came that the first tower had been hit. She had never felt fear like that before, not even the night her aunt came to take her after her parents had died. The fear gripped her whole body like a crushing embrace that shook her to the core. She made a promise to herself in that moment that she would somehow make a difference and would work toward making sure no one ever had to feel what she was feeling as she rode her bike the few short miles to her home in Clayton, North Carolina. Clayton was a small, rather affluent town that always made Tyler feel safe.

That day in September proved that nowhere was truly safe when dealing with the actions of madmen. Her aunt was sitting in the living room watching the TV and gripping the phone in her hand, tears running down her face, when Tyler came in and sat with her. They held each other while they watched the carnage unfold. They didn't receive the official word about her uncle for several days, but her aunt said she knew as soon as it happened. She had felt it somewhere deep in her soul.

It would have been easy for her aunt Claire to fall apart, to lose control, if even for a few weeks. But that never happened. She remained strong and stoic, saying that she owed it to Adam to make the most of her life and to stay focused for Tyler. There was no one in the world Tyler admired more. But at night, when the birds had stopped singing and the wind was the only voice that swam around the outside of the house, Tyler could hear her aunt crying and asking questions of a God that never seemed to answer.

When Tyler told her aunt a year later that she was gay, her aunt had grabbed her and hugged her for several minutes, as tears streamed down Tyler's face and the fear of rejection rattled her body. North Carolina wasn't exactly known for embracing what Tyler had always recognized she was. Her biggest fear had been her aunt's rejection, born of knowing she'd been brought up in a conservative family in a conservative part of the country, more than anything she'd ever said. Tyler carried every word her aunt had said with her when she was alone and scared in war zones and brought them out like a keepsake when she was at her weakest. *Oh, my sweet child, you're perfect just the way you are. The only thing that's new is that I love you more because I can love all of you.*

Tyler wondered if she would ever be as brave again as she was that night with her aunt. Could she ever show anyone again her whole self? And if she could, would they accept her and all the things she'd done? She thought about Brooke. No, she couldn't take the risk. She punched her pillow and tried to get some sleep. No point in wishing for things that weren't meant to be.

CHAPTER FIVE

The room was poorly lit. It irritated Thompson that people would put so little effort into their seemingly lucrative business. He didn't understand how people expected to be taken seriously when they lacked such apparent attention to detail. He watched as the balding, short man chewed on his toothpick while he was looking over the list Thompson had just handed him. A few minutes passed, and Thompson was starting to get annoyed. "It isn't written in Japanese. Can you do it or not?"

The man stopped chewing for a moment and stared at Thompson. When he spoke, his Russian accent was thick. "You are impatient."

Thompson looked at his watch. "And busy."

The man put the piece of paper in his pocket. "I can do this for you. But it won't be cheap."

Thompson motioned around the room. "Obviously. You have a tremendous amount of overhead."

The Russian smiled. He took a small notebook out of his pocket and scribbled, then handed the torn-out piece of paper to Thompson. "I need that amount wired to the account number there, seventy-two hours before the delivery, or you get nothing."

Thompson took the small note, looked at the scribbles, and then stared at the man. "Fine."

The man smacked both hands against his own chest. "Come. You take a drink of vodka with me. Finalize business."

Thompson turned toward the door and walked out. "No."

He returned to his office and notified Mr. Lark that the weapons had been secured. He wasn't thrilled about giving Mr. Lark's money to such an obvious moron, but that couldn't be helped, and the Russian came highly recommended. He put a checkmark next to the "weapons" line item on his to-do list. He loved lists. There was always a sense of accomplishment and completion that came with each little mark. Each aspect needed to be done with precision, accuracy, and without any idiots being involved. *Can't really control that though. Idiots are everywhere.* He lit a cigar, confident he would achieve his desired outcome. He thought briefly about pushing up the date, but then changed his mind. *Perfection can't be rushed.*

He ran through a variety of computer simulations regarding his infiltration into the Farm. The program had been designed to compute all the possible outcomes that could take place. His company had originally designed it to sell to the Department of Defense, but since it was still in its beta testing phases, they weren't fully aware of its capabilities. Hours passed as he input several complex situations that could possibly arise. Once again, thoroughly pleased with himself, he smiled. There was no way anything would be able to stop him. In a time where information was absolute power, he and his employer would be infinitely wealthy. He would also have the opportunity to kill Tyler Monroe, something his brother should have done when he had the chance.

❖

Brooke spent the night tossing and turning in her pitch-black room. Her body had hummed with arousal, confusion, disappointment, and several other emotions she couldn't quite place. She replayed every stomach-flipping, breath-stealing moment. The look in Tyler's eyes, the feel of her body... *I know she felt it too.* Tyler had managed to captivate her, something no one else had ever come close to doing. She wanted to shake some sense into Tyler, nearly as much as she wanted to put her mouth all over her body and learn every inch of skin. *Well, get over it. She made it very clear that was the first and last time.*

Brooke stared at her peeled banana blankly. She was tired, her body was hungry, and she knew that she should eat. Her mind may have been telling her to put the fruit in her mouth, but what she was really hungry for wouldn't be underneath her neatly removed peel. She set it on the table and sighed.

"Are you okay?" Patrick asked, his voice was filled with concern.

"Yeah." Brooke shook herself out of her mood and managed a half smile at Patrick.

"I'm here, Brookie, if you need to talk, if you need anything."

The worry in his eyes unsettled her. "Patrick, I'm really okay, just not sleeping very well. Thank you for always checking on me, though." She placed her head lightly on his arm and continued staring at the rapidly browning fruit.

Brooke's other two classmates were gossiping about Tyler. Speculation, although practiced at the CIA, wasn't something they should be directing at a superior. They speculated about her dating status, her military status, and whether or not she would stay in her teaching position.

Patrick shoved away from the table and stood. "Instead of sitting around gossiping like a bunch of schoolgirls, why don't you two just worry about passing the damn class?" He stormed away and out of the room.

Brooke was taken off guard by his outburst and went after him, leaving her banana and shocked classmates behind.

When she finally caught him in the hallway, she grabbed his shoulder and turned him around. His face was flushed, and he stared at the blue-and-white tiled floor, avoiding eye contact. His eyes were cloudy with anger, and the hands on his hips indicated that he was trying to control himself.

"Hey." Brooke gently touched his arm. "Everything okay, buddy?"

Patrick shook his head. "I'm just so sick of them. I read that report Jennifer was talking about." Patrick leaned back against the wall, seeming to relax. "What happened to the sergeant out there, what happened to her team…that was some horrific stuff. You know, before that mission, they had taken out eleven optimal targets. Gunnery Sergeant was the primary for all of them. She's a damn hero, and they talk about her like the mean girls in high school."

Brooke was always impressed with Patrick's compassion, with his sense of right and wrong, and this time was no different. She placed her hands on his shoulders and forced him to meet her gaze. "You're a good recruit and a great friend. A few more weeks with these knuckleheads and we're out of here. And what they say doesn't change who she is or what she's done. Nothing they say matters."

Tyler came around the corner and hesitated when she saw them, but seemed to lift her chin and kept coming. "Morning."

"Morning, Sergeant. See you in a few hours." Patrick smiled.

Tyler gave him a nod. "Good luck on your testing this morning." She gave Brooke a brief, cold nod and continued past them.

Brooke felt the disappointment smash over her like a ton of bricks. *Last night really didn't mean anything to her. What was I thinking?*

Patrick slid his arm around her shoulder and started moving her down the hallway toward the testing center. "Come on. Let's take turns quizzing each other."

Brooke pulled her thoughts away from Tyler. *Time to concentrate on the reason I'm here.* "Yeah, okay."

The testing they endured every week bordered on mind numbing. It was intended to keep their skills sharp and their minds on par for everything they had learned over the course of their training. Brooke found it redundant and boring. Retaining information and facts was easy. She didn't have a photographic memory, but for all intents and purposes, it may as well have been. She answered the questions without much thought. Her main focus was on Tyler, wondering where she was and what she was doing in that moment. *Probably running. Seems like something she likes to do.* Brooke figured that's where she would go to clear her mind, and what she would perceive as getting back on track.

Brooke finished her test and quickly left the testing center. She hurried over to the women's locker room and changed into her PT clothes.

As Brooke was jogging over, she saw Tyler sitting on the bench, rubbing her calf. The slouch in Tyler's body and the obvious weight on her shoulders tugged at Brooke's heart. She wanted to keep her safe, protect her, and shield her from whatever she was going through. She had never felt like that with anyone before, and she didn't understand why it was happening with a woman who wouldn't even give her a chance. She ran a hand through her hair and made the painful walk over, her heart protesting every step.

"Hey there, Sergeant," Brooke said as blandly as possible.

She positioned herself across from Tyler and took a seat on the ground, leaning her body over to grab her toes and stretch her hamstrings. "Finished testing early and figured I would get a quick run in."

Tyler looked up. "Not getting enough of a workout in class, Hart?" Tyler leaned forward, pulling her bent legs closer to her body.

Her hair fell forward to cover her eyes and Brooke's heart skipped a beat. "Not the case at all. I just enjoy running, and I figured an extra few miles couldn't hurt."

Tyler smiled but stayed silent.

Brooke broke the silence, spontaneously deciding to jump in. "Have a drink with me."

Tyler shook her head slightly. "Have a drink with you? Like go out on a date with you?"

Well, that's not a no. "Yes, have a drink with me. We're allowed to go out. We aren't prisoners here, and tomorrow is our off day." She smiled at Tyler for good measure, a smile she hoped would be impossible to turn down. When Tyler didn't come right out and say no, Brooke realized it was her chance. "We don't have to leave here together. Meet me at MJ's Tavern tonight at twenty-one hundred."

Tyler took a deep breath. "Isn't that place about an hour drive from here?"

Brooke smiled again and tilted her head to the side. "It will be good to get out. Come on."

Tyler blew out a long breath. "One drink, but it's not a date."

Brooke got up, did one last stretch, and said over her shoulder as she set off on her run, "Okay, it's not a date."

❖

Brooke finished her run and jogged back over to the yard, where Jennifer was stretching. "You're here early."

Jennifer studied Brooke for a minute. "You're in a good mood. What gives?"

Brooke didn't answer and Jennifer rolled her eyes. "Okay then, Ms. Talkative, why don't you help me with a few techniques? The sergeant is going to kill me if I don't get these down."

"Sure, I would love to."

Jennifer swung her leg around, clearly meaning to hit Brooke's face, but she missed and ended up off balance. She threw a punch that was blocked, but with no counterpunch to block. The more she missed, and the more Brooke failed to return the punches or kicks, the more Jennifer became frustrated. Her punches and kicks started to flail, and although Brooke tried to talk to her and explain how to do things differently, she seemed deaf to the instruction. She was almost in a blind haze of aggression when Tyler stepped between them.

"You aren't doing her any favors, Hart."

Jennifer bent over, trying to catch her breath, and looking for all the world like she wanted to throw a serious punch at someone.

Brooke shook her head, baffled. "I don't know what you mean, Sergeant."

Tyler looked at her sideways, keeping an eye on Jennifer. "Do you honestly think that Glass will encounter someone in the field that will come at her with less than one hundred percent?"

Brooke shook her arms out. "No, ma'am. But I was trying—"

Tyler put her hands on her hips. "Then don't train that

way. You're setting her up to get hurt, or even worse, in the field."

Brooke heard the finality in Tyler's voice. She understood how real that possibility was in Tyler's world, and a part of her ached for her. Still caught up in thought, Brooke took a solid right hook to the jaw. She stumbled back and hit one knee. She had to rest her hand on the ground to control her dizziness, and when she looked back, Glass was coming at her again. Brooke stood and used Jennifer's own motion against her. *If that's how it needs to be...* With one swift movement, she moved out of the way, hit her between the shoulder blades, and with a swift leg sweep, had her face down on the ground. Brooke pulled her arm behind her back, although she didn't use the kind of force she knew would break her arm.

Tyler smiled down at them. "That, Recruit Hart, is much better."

Jennifer struggled under Brooke and mumbled a few incoherent words before Brooke let her up.

Tyler said, "I'm going to give you all ten minutes to get over to the range. We'll be starting with small weapons and working our way up." They fell back quickly, and when Brooke passed Tyler, she couldn't help but smile at her. Maybe they couldn't be more than friends or, hell, more than student and teacher, but she liked that Tyler pushed her to be her best. And she hadn't missed the way Tyler's eyes had traveled over her body. When Tyler's attention turned to her phone, Brooke jogged off with a smile.

❖

Anxiety formed a lump in Tyler's throat. The message on her phone, from a blocked number, read THERE IS A

BREACH IN SECURITY. That phrase was one that no one sworn to protect others ever wanted to hear or see. The memories of Iraq came flooding back as she broke into a sprint toward the director's office.

By the time she reached Director Broadus's office, the fear had dissipated and her military training had taken over. She needed to isolate the potential threat and act accordingly. She started a mental sequence of events to protect and isolate the Farm from any type of threat. She stopped at Mary's desk, the director's receptionist, whom she had come to know and like. She had a husband, two children, and had retirement aspirations of painting for hours on the beach. Mary didn't bother looking up from her computer while she typed. "Is something on fire?" she teased her.

"I need to speak with the director right away." Although Tyler's voice had come out as controlled and confident, Mary took one look at Tyler and motioned her toward the office.

"I'll clear his next appointment. Go right in."

Tyler managed a brief tap on the side of the desk as thanks and pushed through the heavy oak door to the director's office.

Director Broadus was seated behind his desk reading a report when Tyler came in.

He glanced up at her. "Is something the matter, Sergeant?"

Tyler stood in front of his desk, making sure she controlled her tone and voice as she explained what had happened, starting from the first time she'd had a call from the blocked number. When she had finished explaining everything, she waited silently for his next instruction.

He sat back in his chair and allowed it to swivel from side to side briefly. "Please take a seat." He motioned to the chair.

Tyler sat, although she wanted nothing more than to jump up and *do* something.

"My first question is why this person felt it necessary to contact you. If they were truly concerned about the well-being of this facility, there would be much more effective channels."

Tyler, a bit taken aback by his laid-back attitude, answered, "Not sure, sir."

"I assume that you're well aware of the extraordinary security measures in place at this training facility. And it's not just the guards, cameras, and electric fences; we have a system in place that alerts us if an unknown device is placed into any of the computers, even those that are available for the recruits to email their family members. The likelihood of a breach is virtually nil."

Tyler contemplated his response. "But couldn't one of those be compromised?" She tried to sound steady. She knew that the CIA was known for their arrogant assertiveness and their egos, aspects that sometimes made them good at their jobs, but she had thought the director would have responded differently.

Broadus stared thoughtfully at her. "I'm going to do a sweep of the facility, full-scale. Let's see what turns up."

Tyler's tightened body eased slightly. "I'm available for anything that you need, sir. I can help."

"I have no doubt, Sergeant, and I appreciate it. I'll keep you in the loop. If you get any more information, texts, or calls, come to me immediately. I'm going to add your phone to the security sweep and see if we can come up with anything. My assumption would be that if this person really wants to be undetected, they would use a burner phone. But you never know; we may get lucky."

Tyler nodded her agreement, and the director picked up his desk phone. Realizing that she was being dismissed, she began to walk out the door, but she hesitated before opening it. "Sir, there are moments I wish I could change, take back.

Moments I brushed off as just an uneasy feeling, but those feelings turned out to be right, and now there isn't anything I wouldn't give to make a different decision. I don't know why this person has contacted me instead of someone higher up, but if there's anything to it, I don't want to be the one who didn't do anything about it."

She pushed opened the door, and as she left, she heard the director pick up the phone and say, "I want a full-scale security scan of the facility. I want one done every day at sporadic hours for the next two weeks."

When Tyler reached the range, she was pleased to see that the recruits had continued without her there to supervise. Since they all had basic gun training, they had started to take target practice with standard-issue 9mm sidearms. She was also pleased to see that Carlson was an impressive shot and had obliterated every primary target zone. Brooke gave her a quick glance, and although Tyler wanted nothing more than to talk to her, aware of her surroundings, she decided it would have to wait until later.

Tyler took stock of the weapons that were on site for training purposes. There were more than enough possibilities: sniper rifles, semi-automatic weapons, a variety of sidearms, and of course a vast assortment of knives. Feeling herself settle into the task at hand, she asked the group to come over so they could begin what would be a lengthy lesson in weaponry.

CHAPTER SIX

All it took for Tyler to convince Nicole to let her borrow her car was the promise of breakfast and details regarding her night out, which Tyler had already decided wasn't going to happen.

If she hadn't known she was looking for MJ's Tavern, she would have driven right past it. Tyler had Googled the tavern in order to get an address earlier that day and was surprised when she realized that it was a gay bar. A gay bar in the South wasn't something advertised on billboards up and down the highway. Tyler parked and went inside.

The place was already starting to fill up, and Tyler figured she still had about ten minutes before Brooke arrived, so she ordered a beer and sat at a table, idly watching the baseball game that flashed across one of the many TVs. She wondered for the thousandth time if she was doing the right thing. The thought vanished the moment Brooke walked through the door. The black leather dress that clung to every part of her body looked like it had been made specifically for her. Her chestnut hair fell to her flawlessly sculpted shoulders and seemed to frame her smile to perfection. Tyler was suddenly thirsty, and warm, and drunk with desire.

"Hi." Brooke sounded almost shy.

Tyler managed to string a coherent thought together, but barely. "What can I get you to drink?"

"A beer is fine, thanks."

The contrast was intoxicating. Brooke could walk into a bar looking the way she did and still order a beer. It was just another layer of Brooke that Tyler found desirable. She headed to the bar.

Brooke watched as Tyler ordered her drink and hoped her face wasn't as flushed as she felt it was. She knew she was unbelievably attracted to Tyler, that much was apparent whenever they were anywhere near each other. Seeing each other outside the confines of training was something else entirely. Her dark blue jeans, tight white shirt, and black leather jacket didn't scream instructor; they screamed come put your hands on me. The delicious sense of anticipation was made more intense by the way Tyler had looked at her when she came in, as though she could devour her. Brooke took a deep breath and begged her responses to settle down. She wanted to get to know Tyler, and the desire to drag her into a dark corner wasn't going to help her learn about her. *Well, not that way.*

Tyler came back to the table and slid the frosty mug in front of Brooke. "Is there a reason you picked a spot so far out of the way?"

Brooke was embarrassed by her answer, but she didn't want to lie. "I know you said this wasn't a date...but it is, and I wanted it to feel like one. I knew that if we were closer to Camp Peary, you'd look over your shoulder every five seconds."

Tyler smiled and inclined her head to acknowledge the truth of it. "How did you get out here?"

Brooke shrugged. "I took a cab."

Tyler took her hand. "That's ridiculous. You should have

said you didn't have a way out here. I'll drive you back. I have Nicole's car."

Brooke scrunched her eyes, trying to place who Nicole was.

"Nicole Sable. I believe you had her when you trained in anti-terrorism."

Brooke nodded, a little too relieved. She liked Agent Sable and had learned a great deal from her, and she also knew she was very straight. It seemed like Tyler had read her mind because she squeezed her fingers for reassurance. Brooke again tried to focus on the conversation. "So, why Camp Peary? I'm sure you could have been assigned anywhere."

Tyler seemed to think about her response, something Brooke liked that about her. Tyler wasn't someone who would pepper you with answers or things that you might want to hear. She genuinely considered each question and answer before she spoke.

"I'm not sure that I deserve to be a Marine anymore, but I'm not sure I know how to be anything else. Camp Peary seemed like a good place to try to figure it out."

The statement was made with overwhelming simplicity, and yet it was drenched in pain and confusion. "You don't honestly believe that, do you?" Tyler tried to give her a smile, but the attempt was futile. Brooke rubbed a small circle on Tyler's hand with her thumb, and when she didn't answer, she carried on. "Tyler, I don't think you realize how much we've all learned from you, how much we all respect you."

Tyler stared at the methodical motion on her hand. "What if I can't be a Marine? I'm far away from my normal duty. I may not be what they want anymore." Tyler gazed down at the table, seemingly embarrassed by her question.

"You may be a Marine, but that's not all you are. You're

an amazing woman I want to be around more and more every moment I spend with you."

Tyler's jaw clenched and she laced her fingers through Brooke's. "Dance with me."

Brooke simply nodded.

The small dance floor was a few feet away from a busy pool table, but the change in lighting offered a small sense of intimacy. Brooke fit into Tyler's arms perfectly, and she had to force herself to breathe normally when her body pressed against Tyler's and she felt strong arms come around her waist. The embrace was intoxicating, and Brooke focused on staying in the moment, not wanting to miss a single second. She closed her eyes, trying to burn this moment, this image, into her memory.

Tyler whispered in Brooke's ear, "I like the way this feels."

Brooke put her head on Tyler's shoulder and drank in her fragrance, a smell that was unique to Tyler, an addictive scent of amber and forest. She kissed the side of Tyler's neck softly and moved up the smooth column to the bottom of her ear, and when she felt Tyler's breath catch, she bit down softly. "I'm not sure I can get enough of you." Brooke watched as goose bumps broke out over Tyler's neck. Tyler pulled back, forcing Brooke to look at her. Eyes swimming with need came into focus, and Tyler leaned in, pressing Brooke's mouth to her own.

The kiss wasn't as frantic as it had been before. This time it was slow and teasing. She put her hands on Tyler's neck and pulled her closer, wanting to deepen the kiss so she could drink Tyler in.

Brooke finally broke the kiss and leaned her forehead against Tyler's. "Oh my God." Tyler simply nodded her agreement, her hands sliding up and down the sides of

Brooke's leather dress. She'd nearly decided against wearing it, worrying that it would be too obvious, but the feel of Tyler's hands caressing her body through it made her extremely glad she'd been brave enough to wear it.

They swayed to the music for a while, and Brooke sank into Tyler's embrace. The song ended and another one began, but Brooke had no intention of letting Tyler go. She rested her head on Tyler's shoulder again, enjoying the closeness and allowing herself to believe that this wasn't just for the night. It could be longer, if only Tyler would allow it. She went back to memorizing the way Tyler's hands felt on her, the way she smelled, and the way Tyler's body tightened every time Brooke moved her head and her hair brushed her neck. Brooke hadn't realized that the music had stopped again until Tyler took her hand and led her back over to the table.

Brooke wanted to know everything. She was trying to figure out where to begin, but Tyler beat her to the start line.

"How many times have you been here?"

Brooke shook her head and laughed. "Did you really just pull the 'come here often' line?"

Tyler dramatically hung her head and feigned embarrassment. "I guess I did."

Brooke smiled. "It's okay. I like that I make you nervous."

Tyler looked up at her and gave her a half smile. "I don't know if nervous is the right word."

Brooke was intrigued, and she liked this little game they were playing, so she leaned forward on the table, putting her hand close to Tyler's but not touching it. "What is the right word then, Sergeant?"

Tyler stared at their hands, but she didn't pull away. "Curious."

Tyler made eye contact with Brooke and held the stare. Brooke's body ran hot again, the urge to touch Tyler overwhelming. She put her fingertip on the top of Tyler's hand and ran it down to the end of her middle finger. "We can relieve some of that curiosity."

Tyler seemed to think about it, and then Brooke saw the moment she lost her. Her eyes changed from a stormy blue to guarded. She pulled her hand away. "We can't, Brooke. As much as I want to, I can't."

Brooke's emotions usually ran close to the surface, and had this been any other woman, she would have written her off right then and there. She had no intention of chasing a woman who didn't want her. And yet, Tyler was different. For some reason, she believed her when she said she really wanted to, and that Tyler felt it too, what was happening between them. She also knew that if they were ever going to really have a chance, Tyler would need to feel good about the choice, and pressuring her to move to a place she wasn't comfortable wasn't about to work. "It's okay, Tyler. I understand."

Tyler finally said softly, "Come on. Let me take you home."

The car ride was made in silence. Brooke fought the urge to touch Tyler. Everything in her body was screaming at her to do so, the need was almost primal. Somehow she managed to control the impulse, not wanting to put any more distance between them. She watched her from the passenger seat. "You really are beautiful."

Tyler blushed, smiled, and continued to concentrate on the road.

They arrived back on base, and Tyler dropped Brooke off in front of her barracks. When Brooke reached for the door, Tyler grabbed her hand. Brooke stopped and looked at her. Desire flaring back up, the current that was always present between them flickered under Tyler's fingertips. Brooke waited for Tyler to say something. When nothing came, Brooke picked up the hand that was resting on top of hers and gently kissed it. "Good night, Tyler." Brooke got out of the car and walked into her building, fighting the urge to look back.

❖

Tyler tapped the pen against her leg. She held the receiver up to her ear and concentrated on her breathing.

"Sergeant Monroe, maybe it would be easier if I recommended you to another psychiatrist. One closer to base."

The sweat was beading on the back of her neck. "No. I don't want to have to start over with anyone new."

The doctor paused before urging her on. "Then you have to talk to me."

Tyler didn't want to have to go through the process again. The process of having to reestablish a connection, of explaining herself all over again, to someone new, someone she didn't know if she could trust. But she also didn't want to sit across from someone and have them stare at her while she confessed her sins. She took a deep breath. "The dream came as it always does. It's always so real. The smells, the rush of adrenaline, the confusion, the chaos, the panic. I can never make those stop. This time it started in the beginning though, when we first left for patrol." Tyler let her memories take hold.

She watched as they piled into two Humvees, one after another with their rifles held tightly against their chests. Before the last one got in, he nodded and smiled. "Ladies first." He motioned to the massive vehicle.

"Oh, piss off and get your ass in the Humvee."

He laughed and got in, and she followed.

The sun beat in from the window, and although the

standard-issue sunglasses kept out most of the glare, the sun was unforgiving. Hot, desolate, endless. The inside of the vehicle was filled with chatter of home, teasing banter, and a sense of camaraderie.

Tyler took a deep breath. Remembering the laughter. She always tried to remember the laughter. The dead hills, the sand, the nothingness was there in the background, but when Tyler was awake, she tried to remember the laughter.

"Hey, Top, you going to call that girl when we get back? What was her name again?"

Tyler continued to look out the window. "Shit, Anderson, I don't remember."

He slapped her leg, "Of course you don't." He laughed. "I don't even know why I bother asking."

Then the explosion.

The Humvee shook, the windows blew out, the rolling ensued.

The screams. The damn screams were there all over again. Tyler felt her heartbeat pick up, and she squeezed her leg to remind herself she was in this time, in this moment.

Finally, the psychiatrist pulled her back into the present. "Was there anything different that you woke up feeling this time, Sergeant?"

Tyler was quiet for a moment, not wanting to admit what the difference had been. "Yes. This time, in the dream, there was a face for the woman he brought up. There was a name."

"Oh? You remembered?"

"No. I hadn't met her yet. I met her here, actually. I don't know how she ended up in my dream."

"It's okay, Sergeant. These things aren't always linear. Current situations can manifest themselves in our subconscious. Do you want me to tell me about her?"

Tyler hesitated for a minute, unsure what the doctor's response would be. She decided to tell her the truth, as much of it as she could, anyway. "Her name is Brooke Hart. She's a recruit here at Camp Peary."

"I see. Is there anything else you would like to tell me?"

"I have agreed to see her. Socially."

The silence was only a few seconds, but seemed like minutes. "How does that make you feel? To have plans with a woman you're instructing?"

"I…I don't know."

And that was the scariest thing of all. She let people in, and she failed them. If she let Brooke in, would she fail her too? Even as just a friend?

She hung up with the shrink, more questions than answers giving her a headache.

❖

A few days later, Tyler sat thinking about her night with Brooke. She hadn't wanted to leave the moment. She had wanted to stay wrapped in Brooke's arms, a realization which was not only unsettling, it was terrifying. She thought back to that night she had lain in bed, wondering if she could ever be the person that Brooke needed and deserved. She'd started to panic, and her ever-present self-doubt was like poison pumping through her bloodstream. Questioning every emotion, every decision. Brooke deserved so much more than what Tyler was capable of offering.

Now, she sat in a booth at the local bar, the hum of the neon signs an almost soothing annoyance. The chatting of strangers and old friends surrounded her, and the mixture of Top 40 and Old Rock blended in to make a perfect cliché picture of the neighborhood bar. A week had passed since Tyler had first gone to see the director, and she hadn't heard anything more, nor had she received any more strange texts or calls.

She had gone through her day-to-day regimen of training the recruits, managing to steal glances at Brooke, but she kept their interaction to a minimum, unable to move forward and unwilling to hurt Brooke by not being the person she deserved. She saw the look of hurt in Brooke's eyes, but turned away from it. She'd get over it easier now than if they pursued it and it ended in some kind of super lesbian drama.

Her thoughts were scattered, split between what she felt was impending danger from an unknown source, and trying to make sense of her feelings for Brooke. She listened politely to Nicole and Kyle talk about their upcoming vacation, but nothing was truly registering in her head.

When Kyle went to try to scrape up a game of pool with someone he had recognized, Nicole moved over and sat next to Tyler. "Everything okay?" Nicole asked, slightly pushing into Tyler's side.

"Yeah." Tyler sipped her drink slowly. "Just caught up in my own thoughts, I guess." Tyler wanted to explain what she was thinking, about Brooke as well as the possible security breach. After all, they should be privy to it as well. If something happened, it would affect all of them, right? That wasn't Tyler's call to make though. If the director wanted everyone involved, he would have involved them.

"You want to talk about last Saturday night and where you went with Brooke Hart?"

Nicole had been begging for information every morning since then, claiming that she needed to live vicariously through Tyler. Tyler knew she was teasing, because the intensity between Nicole and Kyle could be felt by everyone within a ten-foot radius. Tyler trusted Nicole, trusted her enough to tell her that it was Brooke she had been with, but what had happened between them wasn't something Tyler was ready to share. It was too precious, and too painful. She shook her head and Nicole patted her arm understandingly.

"There's that little redhead." Nicole motioned over to the bar where the woman Tyler had met previously was staring at her. The woman gave a small flirtatious wave, obviously arching her back slightly.

Tyler felt herself slightly blush. "I don't really have time for that right now." She didn't say that no one would ever live up to the imprint Brooke had left deep down, in a place no one had ever touched.

"Ha!" Nicole said loudly. "You probably have more free time now than you ever did in the Marines." Nicole gave her a wicked grin. "Even you need to blow off steam sometimes. Why not her?"

Tyler looked intently at the redhead and then shook her head. "Not really my type." She started to peel the label from her beer bottle to hide her reaction. The truth was that the woman was exactly her type—beautiful, small, and she shared the need for a brief interlude, not a long-term commitment. *And then along came Brooke.* Now there was nothing she could do during her day to prevent her from thinking of her.

Nicole gave Tyler an intense stare. "This wouldn't have anything to do with Brooke, would it?"

That's it. I'm literally going to throw up right here. Tyler knew she was probably the color of her aunt's prize-winning tomatoes. She wanted to deny what was happening, what she felt, but lying about Brooke wasn't something she felt comfortable doing. "Brooke is special."

Nicole smiled as she sipped her beer. "Without question." After a moment, Nicole leaned closer to Tyler. "So what's the problem?"

Tyler couldn't possibly explain the intricacy of her emotions. That she felt as though she weren't whole anymore, that she wouldn't ever be good enough for anyone, let alone the woman constantly occupying her mind. She gave the easy answer, the answer that should have stopped her in her tracks from the moment she met Brooke, the answer that should have kept her from ever putting a single finger on Brooke. "She's a recruit. Off limits."

Nicole nodded thoughtfully. "She is, but she's also an adult and she won't be a recruit forever."

Tyler shifted in her seat. "No, but she is one now. And I won't go there."

Nicole gave Tyler a friendly squeeze. "Just be careful not to shut doors before you even open them."

Kyle walked back up flashing the twenty dollars he'd won from his game of pool.

Tyler continued to stare at her bottle of beer as if it held the answers to all of the world's issues, when she heard Kyle say, "Isn't that Patrick Bowing and Brooke Hart?" Tyler's stomach jumped into her chest, and Nicole's face lit up.

She swatted Tyler's hand. "Would you look at that… speak of the devil."

Tyler gave her a look that asked her not to say anything more. Somehow, it being said out loud around other people made the whole situation feel that much worse.

Tyler needed some space. She wasn't used to having things unfold without a prior plan in place. She pushed herself out of the booth and headed toward the bathroom, when the redhead stopped her in her tracks. Tyler, who had been focusing on getting out of Brooke's line of sight, looked at her a little dazed.

The woman gave her a seductive grin and ran her hand up

Tyler's arm and around her neck. "Did I put that dizzy look on your face?"

Tyler was trying to think past the desire to run. "Uh, I wasn't expecting to see you again."

The woman ran her hand through Tyler's hair. "I told you to find me here. This isn't just a coincidence, is it?"

Tyler was acutely aware of Brooke's presence and managed a quick glance in her direction. Brooke was gripping the pool stick, and Tyler couldn't be completely sure, but her knuckles looked white.

Tyler removed the woman's hand with a mumbled apology and escaped into the bathroom. She splashed some cold water on her face and took several deep breaths. Her leg ached slightly, and she desperately wanted to escape back to her lodgings. *Talk to her. Don't ignore her like she's not worth even the courtesy of a hello. Idiot.*

Tyler glanced around the bar as she made her way back to the table, but didn't see the only person she wanted to.

Nicole shrugged slightly. "They left."

Tyler nodded, trying to convince herself that she was relieved and not disappointed. "Oh, okay."

Nicole grabbed Kyle's arm. "Come on, tiger. Take me home."

Kyle's eyes lit up. "Yes, ma'am!"

They got back to the Farm about ten minutes later, and Tyler said good night to her friends. She watched the car drive off and momentarily felt a pang of jealousy. Not because she envied either one of them, but because she envied what they had found in each other. This feeling in and of itself was entirely foreign, and she knew Brooke was the reason for the change. She absently walked back to her barracks, rubbing her arms to try to push away the night chill.

Tyler was walking through the darkened structures when a hand grabbed her and pulled her into a corner. Before she could get out a word of protest, Brooke's mouth was on hers, fiercely claiming Tyler as her own. Tyler's body reacted. She wanted to be dominated and claimed. Brooke's hands were under her shirt, scratching at her back and leaving a scorched trail in her wake. The small amount of pain it brought almost sent Tyler over the edge.

Brooke pushed her into the wall, biting and nipping at every exposed area. She managed to get a single sentence out. "I don't like seeing anyone else with their hands on you."

What would have normally sent up a red flag for Tyler turned her on even more. A pool of wetness throbbed between her legs at Brooke's claim. She put her hands in Brooke's hair and put every ounce of desire, need, and devotion into her kiss. A set of passing voices forced them into a brief moment of clarity, and Brooke leaned into Tyler. Without saying another word, she kissed Tyler one more time and then disappeared back around the side of the building.

CHAPTER SEVEN

Thompson had finally narrowed it down to three scenarios that had a success rate of eighty-five percent. He flipped through the first folder and tossed it to the side once he saw the words "aerial attack." There was no way that was going to happen. The Farm was a restricted air space, and setting something like that up would be needlessly costly.

The next required the placement of several snipers in the area. He momentarily contemplated the idea, but again, tossed it aside. *Too many casualties.* It wasn't that he was opposed to seeing these people with bullets in their heads. He didn't really care who died. The problem was that it would bring security forces down on them harder and faster than he wanted to deal with.

The last scenario was simple, almost elegant. Thompson grinned. He sent out a text message requesting the few supplies he didn't already have on hand. They would be there in time for the mission. He grabbed the folder and walked down the three flights of steps to the secure garage that dignitaries used when they were in the city. He knew the schedule, and the garage wasn't scheduled to be used again until several weeks after his plan had been executed. He opened the secure door with a PIN code that he'd assigned to an employee who never existed. This room was the temporary home for his supplies and held all the hopes he had envisioned for this conquest.

Thompson practically salivated as he looked over the equipment he would be taking Friday night. He was sure they had everything they could possibly need: night vision goggles, radios, assault rifles, smoke bombs, flash bombs, sidearms, and knives for close attacks. The Farm primarily focused on surveillance for their security measures, and with surveillance no longer being an issue because of the computer infiltration, detailed in the folder he held in his hand, there were only a few guards that stood in his way. He planned on taking them out with tranquilizer darts and replacing their posts with his own men so that nothing would look off from a distance. As much as he wished it were different, killing was never really silent, no matter what they showed in the movies. Tranq darts would drop them quietly. He was also able to obtain voice software that would mimic the CIA guard voices for check-in if the need were to arise.

He knew precisely where Monroe's quarters were located. A simple dart would knock her out and allow him to bring her out of the facility to a holding area he'd designed just for her. He would be in and out in a matter of thirty minutes, and no one would know until it was far too late. It was the perfect plan. Lark would get what he wanted and Monroe would have a long, painful death. He sent a group text message. "Twenty hundred hours. The agreed upon Friday. Location Two." He sent the message and dropped the phone into the glass of water on a table.

❖

Brooke's attraction to Tyler only deepened. Being with her every day, learning from her, watching her take a bunch of so-called computer hacks and turn them into agents, made Brooke respect her all the more. And with that respect came intense, heavy desire. Since the night behind Tyler's building, they hadn't been alone, and that frustrated Brooke. She decided that once this session was over, she was going to put everything she had into convincing Tyler to give them a chance.

Brooke was the first to cross the finish line of the course that they had practiced on diligently for the last several weeks. This go-round was their final time. She turned to watch her classmates complete it as well. Patrick was only a few seconds behind her, then Jennifer. Chris Carlson was the last to finish, but still within the allotted time frame. None of them were as out of breath as they'd been when they started training, and Brooke felt a small amount of pride in that.

Tyler addressed them. "This Thursday begins your final exam. It will be a mission scenario that will last four days and three nights." She briefly paused to make eye contact with each of them. "It will be full-scale, mission objectives, hand-to-hand combat skills, weaponry—everything that we have covered for the last five weeks. You're all ready for this. You've trained hard and pushed yourselves. I'll be there to observe, but I won't be participating in the scenario. It will be up to all of you to plan your objectives based upon mission status."

Brooke looked around and saw excitement and fear, the exact emotions needed to succeed. Emotions surged through her.

"Everyone get some rest tonight and tomorrow, and then muster here at zero six hundred on Thursday." Tyler gave a final nod and walked out, leaving them to discuss their impending test.

"I still think Hart should be team leader," Patrick said with his arms crossed, looking at each person.

"What a shock, Bowing. You want your girlfriend to be in charge." Jennifer threw the accusation at Patrick like it was an object, her tone as sharp as her last name.

"Do you have a better suggestion?" Chris asked Jennifer.

Patrick held his hands up for silence. "We can't start fighting already, and we need each other to make this work and get through this. Brooke is the best fit, but she needs to want to do it."

Brooke nodded. "I'll happily accept, but it has to be okay with everyone."

Everyone looked at Jennifer, who threw her hands up in the air. "Yeah, okay, Hart is the right person for the job. Of course she is."

Brooke looked around at her tired peers. "Okay then, let's get some sleep like Sergeant said and meet back here tomorrow at ten hundred hours for some practice."

Jennifer stomped off toward their barracks, and Patrick moved off a little way, clearly waiting for Brooke. Chris lingered for a moment, staring at Brooke. "Something on your mind, Carlson?"

He looked like he wanted to say something. His stare was intense and contemplative, but he snapped out of it and walked away. "See you tomorrow, Brooke."

Brooke watched him, wondering what had just taken place. She fought off the feeling that lingered in her stomach that something was off with him. *Probably just nerves.*

When Brooke walked up to Patrick, he said quickly, "Sorry about that back there."

They headed toward their barracks. "About what?"

"Jennifer saying you were my girlfriend."

Brooke let out an exasperated laugh. "If I got upset over everything Jennifer Glass said to provoke me, I'd be in a constant state of disarray."

Patrick stopped walking momentarily, and Brooke stopped to look back at him.

"You could, you know." Patrick looked from side to side and put his hands in his pockets. "Be my girlfriend."

Brooke's heart hurt for Patrick. *We should have had this talk a long time ago.* "Patrick, I love you, but I'm not attracted to men."

Patrick looked at her, and she could almost see his heart breaking.

"Yeah, I kind of got that idea, but you can't blame me for trying."

Brooke kissed his cheek. "If by some random act of God I ever end up in a position where I've switched teams, there is no one else for me but you."

Patrick gave her a sad smile and started walking again. "I hope she knows how lucky she is."

"Who?" Brooke asked.

"The sergeant."

Brooke looked at the ground, focusing on not allowing the emotion in her voice to show. "I don't know what you're talking about."

Patrick gave her a sideways smile. "Brookie, it's written all over your faces, in your body language, even the way you two talk to each other. You do realize that we've been together at the most exclusive, clandestine training facility in the world for the past year? Give me a little credit."

Brooke decided to say nothing instead of lying. Patrick picked up on the lack of response and dropped the topic as well. Luckily, they reached their barracks shortly after.

"See you tomorrow morning," Brooke called out as she walked up her steps. Patrick gave a wave and continued on to his building.

Brooke decided to enjoy the spring evening rather than go

inside just yet. She sat on her steps and started to replay the conversation she'd had with Patrick. *Are we that transparent to everyone?* A few moments into her reflection, Tyler came jogging up the path. She slowed when she reached Brooke and took the earbuds out. She was wearing USMC shorts and a black sports bra, and Brooke had to focus on keeping her hands on her knees so she wouldn't wipe the straggling hairs out of Tyler's face or run her hands up the flexed stomach muscles that were moving rapidly with each breath.

"Hey," Tyler said, panting, "I was actually looking for you."

"Well, you found me." Brooke tried to sound as relaxed and casual as possible, but she was worried that the thoughts and possibilities flooding her brain would burst right out of her.

"I assume that you're team leader."

"I'm not sure why you would assume that, but yes, I am." *Damn, she came to talk to me about work.*

"Good. That's the right decision." Tyler shifted nervously back and forth, examining her shoes. "I know we need to talk," she said softly.

Brooke watched Tyler sift through her thoughts, and her pulse raced. *Please, please say what I want to hear.*

"It's not that I don't have feelings for you, Brooke, because I do. Feelings that I find myself having to work to control."

"Feelings aren't meant to be controlled, not feelings like this."

"It's not that easy for me. I'm new to all of this, not just this teaching gig, but to having feelings that last beyond a few days with a woman. If that long."

Brooke wanted desperately to reach out and touch her, believing that the electricity between them could be conveyed with such a simple gesture. She wanted Tyler to feel their chemistry and understand it was special. She kept her hands in her lap.

"I've never been anything but a Marine. It's what I am good at, who I am, but the person I am right now, standing here in front of you...I barely recognize her."

"I don't know how many times I have to tell you this, you may be a Marine, Tyler Monroe, but there is much more to you than just that. In case you haven't noticed what you've accomplished over the last several weeks, I'll remind you. You took four people who have never even so much as thrown a punch and taught them how to protect themselves in the most extreme of circumstances. You did that with the patience and caring that most people would never be able to harness. You taught us that we're capable, not just desk jockeys. You're so much more than one thing."

Tyler shook her head. "The things I've done, things I should have prevented...I'm not good enough for you, Brooke, and beyond that, I'm dangerous, a liability. I still relive the moment, you know...I don't always know where I am."

Brooke put her hands on her hips. "Now wait a minute, Sergeant. You're the most courageous, ethical, devoted person I know. What happened to your team wasn't, and isn't, your fault."

Tyler shrugged, clearly not convinced. "What if you're wrong? Do you really want to take that chance? Do I?"

Brooke grabbed Tyler's wrists and held them tightly, afraid that if she let go, Tyler would disappear. "What if you're the one that's wrong?"

Tyler stared at Brooke for a long moment, her eyes searching Brooke's, before she pulled away. "I can't take that chance with you, Brooke. I won't risk your feelings like that."

Brooke tried to take Tyler's hands again. "How can we not risk it?" She pointed at Tyler and then to herself. "This is worth a risk."

Tyler practically whispered her final denial. "I can't, Brooke. I just can't."

Brooke's eyes began to well up, and she turned to go up her steps, needing to remove herself from the situation. She didn't want Tyler to see her cry. She wanted to be strong. She wanted to be the person she knew Tyler needed her to be, even if Tyler didn't want her.

"Good night, Sergeant."

CHAPTER EIGHT

B rooke walked down the steps of her building on Wednesday morning feeling as though she were walking through mud. The sky seemed a little dimmer, the air was thicker, and her chest burned with loss. Tyler had left a hole in her heart the night before, and it was still searing this morning. She was beginning to get aggravated with herself. She needed to focus, to get her mind straight. She had worked too hard to derail her training. She wasn't going to let the fact that it hurt to move every part of her body stop her from finishing.

She was surprised when she got to the yard and realized that she was the last person there. They appeared locked in a deep discussion as she approached.

Jennifer, in her normal cocky stance, looked Brooke up and down as if Brooke had forgotten to put her clothes on that morning.

"Everything okay?" Brooke asked as she made her way into the group. Patrick gave her an awkward look that made her even more nervous.

"Let's just get to it, boss. Some of us aren't guaranteed to pass this class." Jennifer had a way of accusing people without actually saying the words.

"What is that supposed to mean?" Brooke tried to leash her anger, but she was just about fed up with Jennifer's antics.

Jennifer took a step closer, getting into Brooke's personal space. "Tell us, Hart. Is the gunnery sergeant as good in bed as she is with a rifle?"

Her tone was meant to be cruel and the words stung, not because Brooke was embarrassed but because she was worried about where Jennifer was going with her comments. *Tyler was right. People talk.* "I don't know what you're talking about, Glass, but I assure you I'm not sleeping with our instructor."

Jennifer gave a small huff. "Not what it looked like from my window last night."

Brooke could feel her cheeks turning a dark red. "Are you accusing me of something? And are you referring to us speaking outside my barracks while she was out jogging? That implies sex to you?" Brooke pushed her finger against Jennifer's chest, hoping she'd take a swing.

Patrick moved between them. "Everyone needs to just calm down. This isn't any of our business. Jen, let's just get to work."

Jennifer looked Brooke up and down one more time before she walked away, and Patrick and Chris followed, leaving Brooke standing there alone.

❖

Tyler watched from a distance as the recruits argued back and forth. Whatever was going on between them would surely have an impact on the impending test mission. She had to forcibly stop herself from going over to intervene, although when she saw Jennifer get in Brooke's face, it took all her willpower to stay put. When Brooke didn't back down, Tyler smiled and relaxed. Brooke could handle herself. She needed to keep her distance and let them work out how to be a team.

She made her way into the mess hall to meet Nicole for

breakfast. She was hurting in a way she couldn't compare to any physical injury she had ever endured. This pain started in the depths of her soul and worked its way through her whole body, as though she'd been poisoned. The loss of her team was a pain she could pinpoint, a moment of horror and terror where she lost nearly everything. She knew the exact cause and she kept it close to her heart. This poison, this loss, ran through her heart in an entirely different way.

"I know the food here is pretty awful, but there was nothing served this morning that accounts for the look on your face."

Tyler continued to push the food around on her plate. "I'm sorry. I'm not very good company."

Nicole dismissed her remark with a wave of her hand. "Seriously, what's going on?"

Tyler wanted to talk to someone, but she couldn't quite fuse the words together to convey what she was feeling. "I told Brooke we could never be together."

Nicole inclined her head slightly and frowned. "Why did you do that?"

Tyler rubbed her temples. "She deserves better, Nicole. She deserves someone that can give themselves over completely."

"You don't think you can do that?"

Tyler shook her head. "I can't because I'm not whole. And I don't know that I ever will be."

"I see." Nicole paused for a moment. "Do you think you're being fair to Brooke?"

Tyler looked up from her plate of congealed food. "What do you mean? I think I'm being more than fair. I'm making sure I don't hurt her."

Nicole sighed. "You took the decision away from her, Tyler. You decided what was best for her without asking what she wanted, or what she could handle. Did you ever think that maybe she wants you just the way you are and that it's okay if you're a little beat up and broken?"

Tyler couldn't think of a response.

"In order to be whole again, you need to be able to feel love. But even more than that, you need to forgive yourself. Let yourself off the hook for things that weren't ever in your control."

Tyler stared at her plate, unable to meet Nicole's penetrating stare. "I always manage to lose the people I love most."

Nicole leaned back in her seat. "So, is it you or Brooke you're really trying to protect?"

Tyler squeezed her eyes shut, trying to block out the pain that washed over her again and again. Her uncle, her team, and now Brooke. She couldn't take any more.

❖

Brooke made the decision not to let Jennifer's accusations get the best of her, not today when she was already feeling vulnerable. She just needed to make it through a few more days, then she would be rid of her for good. It wasn't that she was bothered that her peers had picked up on her interest in Tyler, it was that they were trying to make it out to be something it wasn't, something dirty and forbidden. She'd taken them through various drills, and by the end, they'd all been so exhausted there hadn't been any energy for conversation. They'd gone their separate ways, and Brooke had been grateful for the respite.

She walked down to the small man-made lake on the outskirts of the Farm, a place she didn't get to often, but a nice place to clear her head and help her get some focus. Since the Farm itself was entirely surrounded by forest, she could almost convince herself that she was away somewhere at a resort, instead of at one of the most controlled intelligence training facilities in the world. The spring sun kissed her skin, and she could feel the prickles of the warmth sliding over her arms. Brooke loved the heat on her skin. It reminded her of a portion of her life she spent on base in San Diego, when her father was stationed there. A simpler time, when she wasn't worried about wanting a woman she couldn't have. She lay on her side in the grass and watched the lake water lick the shore in front of her.

Patrick sat next to her. "Hey, troublemaker."

Brooke snorted and looked at him. "I can't believe the nerve of that girl."

"Don't let her get to you. We have bigger fish to fry, and it's none of her business."

"Is this where you get all big brother like on me?"

Patrick gave her a soft shove. Brooke purposely overacted and smiled at him.

"It sure is. I'd offer to beat her up, but I know you can take her."

Brooke continued to stare at the water, trying to puzzle it all out. "I really like her, Patrick." It hurt a little bit every time she thought the words.

"Then let's kick this mission's ass so you can get on with it."

Brooke leaned her head against his shoulder, thankful that she had a friend and teammate like him. "She doesn't want me."

Patrick shook his head. "I don't believe that for one second. Who wouldn't want you?"

She wiped away a stray tear that was slowly moving down her cheek. "She told me I was better off without her. That she wouldn't risk it."

He scoffed softly. "Sounds to me like she's scared, and there's a big difference between being scared and not wanting you."

Brooke sniffled. "I don't know what to do. I can't force her to want me. Or to take a chance, whatever it is."

Patrick shook the shoulder she was leaning on. "That doesn't sound like the Brooke I know."

"What do you mean?"

"Well, the Brooke I know fights for what she wants. Always and without fail. Sometimes people need to know they're worth fighting for."

After a few moments, Brooke sat up and pulled him into a tight hug. "Thank you."

❖

Tyler glanced at her watch. 0600. She loved this time of morning. Even nature felt like it was still asleep. The air was brisk, clean, and the darkness of the night was just starting to show the barest hints of the changing day. But even on such a perfect morning, she couldn't banish the feeling she had deep in her gut of impending danger. As she loaded various supplies into the jeep and double-checked her gear, she remembered a morning very similar to this several months ago. That day ended with her entire team dead, leaving her to feel the guilt of not perishing with them.

She pushed back the welling tears and continued with her preparations. The nightmares were still there, still shaking her awake at night, still draining her energy and messing with her perception. She decided the feeling of danger was a throwback to that moment and did her best to dismiss it. She needed to use the tools her doctor had given her to stay in this moment. She took a deep breath and focused on the redundancy of the task at hand. If something were going on, the director would have done something about it.

Brooke was the first to arrive, wearing her black BDUs, a tight black T-shirt, and had her hair pulled away from her face. When she saw Tyler, she rewarded her with a dimpled smile that melted Tyler's hardened, battle-ready attitude.

"Don't look at me like that," Brooke said.

Brooke brushed a loose strand of hair out of her eyes, and Tyler shivered at the light touch. "Like what?"

Brooke shoved her hands into her pockets and shifted her weight, looking like a nervous teenager. "Like you want to devour me right here, right now."

Tyler leaned against the jeep and took a deep breath, trying to steel herself. "We already had this conversation, Brooke. We can't do this."

Brooke took a step closer. "Correction." She poked Tyler in the chest. "*You* said we can't do this. I don't remember ever getting to voice my opinion."

Tyler pulled her fatigue hat out and pulled it firmly over her head, tucking her hair behind her ears. "I'm really trying to do what is best for you. You've got no idea what I'm like. When the memories hit, and I...I just...fuck."

Brooke took another step closer, so they were within a few inches of one another. "I already have a mother, Sergeant. I'm a grown-up. I decide what's best for me and what I can handle."

Tyler was watching Brooke's mouth move as she spoke, and she desperately wanted to kiss her. "You can't possibly think I would be best for you. You don't know what you'd be in for. What I could do."

Brooke smiled sadly. "I know how I feel when I'm around you, or near you. I know I can tell when you walk into a room, even if I can't see you, I know that the very sound of your voice eases me in a way I've never known. I know that you're hurting and all I want is to make it better."

Tyler made a move to get by her, and Brooke put her hand on her chest, stopping her. "I'm not giving up on you."

"Brooke, today of all days, you need to concentrate. We can talk about us later. Maybe. If there's anything to talk about." She tugged on her hat in frustration. "But damn, today you need to be clear, focused. I won't be there to help you, and you're leading a team. This thing between us, it should be your last thought today."

Patrick's voice filtered through to them through the morning air as he strode up to them. "Brooke? Are you ready?"

Brooke stepped back, putting space between herself and Tyler. "Just loading up the equipment," she yelled back, never taking her eyes off Tyler.

When neither of them acknowledged him and the silence became unbearably awkward, Patrick finally said, "The others are heading out. We should probably get ready."

"Good luck today, both of you." Tyler nodded at Patrick as she moved past them.

Silence hung between Patrick and Brooke as she watched Tyler walk away. Brooke understood with a crushing realization that Tyler owned her heart, whether she wanted it or not.

"I didn't mean to interrupt anything, Brookie. Sorry about that."

Brooke forced her body into motion. She bumped Patrick and smiled. "Let's get to work."

"Roger that, ma'am."

Jennifer and Chris were waiting for Brooke and Patrick. They looked like a team, a team ready for their final test; everyone wore black BDUs and boots, and they all looked more confident than when they'd first started this training. They were ready.

Tyler walked up and they fell into line, standing at attention. Tyler examined each of them. "Recruit Hart."

Brooke stepped forward.

"In this envelope is your mission objective. There is only one rule: you don't leave the confines of the Farm. We will be in the wooded area, but no one is to leave the fenced perimeter. There are no other directions, hints, tips, or any other information to assist you. I'll be coming along as a silent watcher. Although I'll be with you the whole time, I cannot offer assistance or ideas."

Brooke took the envelope from her hand and fell back into line with her classmates.

"Is everyone clear?"

In unison, they responded, "Yes, ma'am."

"Good, then let's get going."

CHAPTER NINE

The mission wasn't a complicated one. The team was to infiltrate a safe house, gain access to a secured computer network, obtain a number of listed files, and then leave a tracing virus in their wake. While Patrick drove, Chris pulled out the map and listed the various places he thought would be an appropriate distance to set up camp away from the target. Glass was studying the mission objectives, and Brooke watched her. She couldn't for the life of her figure out exactly what she had done to make her so angry. Brooke had always been supportive and nurturing to all of her classmates, and Jennifer's attitude was both insulting and confusing.

"What do you think, Hart?"

Chris's question pulled Brooke away from her contemplation and back to where her focus should be, on the mission. "I think that we should set up camp at least half a klick away from the safe house. Find a place with good cover, away from any roads and trails."

Chris nodded and continued to pore over the map, giving directions to Patrick when necessary.

Patrick pulled the jeep over in a heavily tree-covered area. Everyone got out of the vehicle, pulled out their equipment, and then proceeded to cover the jeep with a camouflage tarp, along with tree and bush coverings. They would make the rest of their way to camp on foot.

Brooke loaded her gear onto her back and caught a glimpse of Tyler doing the same. The only difference was, Tyler seemed to be in a zone, performing a task she had probably done several hundred times, in genuine life-or-death situations, whereas Brooke could feel every nerve in her body, even though she knew there was no actual danger of death. She and the other three recruits had been preparing for this mission for the last several years and, overall, the success of it was her responsibility. *Oh God, please don't throw up.*

Carlson went first to scout the prospective area for any signs that something was out of the ordinary, or if there had been security measures put into place to deter intruders. He silently signaled to Hart that he had found something. The group moved up beside him as he pointed to cameras that were sporadically placed throughout the trees. Glass came up beside Carlson and signaled for one of the containers to be brought over to her. She opened the overly large case and pulled out a small unit that looked like a television with a handle coming out from the bottom. She placed the earphones over her head and spent almost two minutes manipulating a variety of frequencies until she found what she was looking for.

Brooke glanced over Glass's shoulder and saw the images that the cameras were taking come into focus. By following the images on the screen, they would be able to avoid the different surveillance cameras and the directions they were pointing. Tyler had taught them that the best thing to do was leave as much in place as possible to avoid detection. Brooke was glad they'd all been paying attention.

The team trudged up the side of the small hill with precision and patience. The sun really beat down on them, and Brooke could feel the sweat dripping down her back. They'd be at their desired location soon, and she wanted to make sure everyone hydrated before they advanced to the next part of their plan. She looked behind and noticed that Jennifer was slightly struggling with one of the larger cases she was lugging up the incline. Brooke hurried over and offered her help.

"No thanks, Hart. I can take care of myself."

"We're a team, Glass. Let me help you."

Glass shook her head. "You can help me by fucking off."

Brooke had to bite her tongue in response. She left Jennifer at the back and took her place again behind Carlson.

Carlson stopped when they reached a secluded portion of the hill and pointed to a grouping of thick brush. Brooke looked around briefly and instructed the team to set up temporary camp. They'd be able to do quite a bit of surveillance from this location and stay reasonably well hidden. Carlson and Brooke set about the task of fastening the brush tarps to give them cover, while Bowing and Glass started setting up their computer network and surveillance system.

Brooke walked over to look at the computer monitors placed under the canopy and laid out the map on the table. Her team gathered around, sipping on canteens.

"I think our best course of action is for a pair of us to take a first run at the complex. We'll be able to set up the infrared pin cameras at each of the access points, place the emergency jammers, and possibly set up a few long-distance microphones. Two people can stay back, one to monitor our signals and the other to stand watch in case the complex sends out scouts." Brooke pointed at the various points of the map and made sure to make eye contact with each of the team, so she was sure they understood what she was saying.

The team seemed to nod in agreement, although Jennifer looked pained by it. Brooke marked two different locations on the map. "I think these are the best places to try to place the equipment, but once we get down there, use your judgment if you think there is a better location." She folded her arms across her chest and continued to stare at the map. "Glass and I will take care of the placement. Bowing, monitor the equipment and make sure we have a good signal. Carlson, you take the first watch, and we'll use the standard two-hour increments. Let's get all of our gear packed, and we'll head down at sunset. Until then, monitor all movements, document everything." Brooke looked at her watch. "It's only oh nine hundred. We still have nine hours until sunset. That's plenty of time to acclimate ourselves."

The team dispersed and started packing their gear. Carlson grabbed his binoculars and rifle and put the earpiece into his left ear.

"Check in every ten minutes," Brooke said to him as he was making his final adjustments, without looking up from the map.

"Roger that." He set off into the trees.

They got camp set up and went about packing their gear and setting up the monitors. Tyler walked over to Brooke's side and stared at the map with her. "What do you think?"

Tyler studied the markings without saying a word for what seemed to Brooke to be several minutes. "I told you, I can't get involved." Brooke realized that Tyler wouldn't give her an answer. She was the only one physically on site with her team, but everything was being monitored back at the facility. And although they couldn't hear their normal conversations without the radio being activated, she knew Tyler wouldn't take the chance of interfering.

Brooke thought briefly that she might be able to gauge Tyler's thoughts through facial expressions. "So you think it's the wrong approach?" Brooke felt a wave of panic and walked around the other side of the table to view the map from another angle. She glanced up at Tyler, whose face remained unchanged.

"I think you're the right person for the job and whatever you decide to do will be okay."

"That was very cryptic of you, Gunnery Sergeant." Brooke shoved her hands in her pockets to keep from reaching out.

Tyler continued to look at the map. "You can plan everything down to the last detail, but remember to be flexible. Things can change in an instant, and you don't want to be so focused on what you planned to do that you aren't able to do what needs to be done."

"Maybe you should take your own advice." Brooke's tone conveyed her aggravation with Tyler's decision regarding their relationship. She knew she shouldn't be thinking about that now, but with Tyler so close to her, it was almost impossible not to.

Tyler walked over to the monitors to see what Bowing was setting up, not taking Brooke's bait.

Patrick was testing the surveillance equipment that Glass and Brooke would take with them to set up when Brooke came up beside him, trying her best to ignore Tyler's presence.

"You ready, Bowing?"

"Always, ma'am." Patrick gave her the smile that warmed her chest with feelings of friendship and loyalty. She looked up at the darkening sky. The day was coming to a close, and her real test was about to start. She pulled her pack up onto her back and checked the straps, her sidearm, her earpiece, and her goggles. Bowing gave her a thumbs-up as she passed him.

Glass was waiting for her and gave her a perfunctory nod.

"I've marked all camera locations for our trek to the complex. We'll need to stay together until we can get down there. Once we separate, check back with camp and they'll be able to help you get through the last part. As soon as your equipment is placed we'll meet back at the dividing location and come back up together."

Jennifer was liberally wiping camouflage paint on her face, which she handed to Brooke when she was done. "Better to be safe than sorry."

They were finishing up when Tyler walked up beside them. Brooke was torn between being glad she was there and wanting to shake some sense into her.

"Good luck," she said before moving back over to the monitors.

❖

Brooke glanced at her watch. They were making good time, and despite the loathing she could often feel radiating from Jennifer's body, it seemed that Jennifer was also willing to put those feelings aside in order to complete the mission. Jennifer slowed as a few lights came into view in the distance. By this time, they were engulfed in natural darkness and would need to don their night vision goggles for the remainder of their mission. As they were kneeling by the tree arranging the sets, Brooke motioned with her hands that they would be splitting at this point. She drew an X on the ground with her finger, and when Jennifer nodded her understanding that this was where they'd meet, Brooke wiped the X away. She motioned that Jennifer should go left, and she'd take the right.

As they headed their separate directions, the radios came to life. Back at camp, their tracking devices told the rest of the team where they were, and Bowing was giving directions to both Brooke and Glass, regarding where the cameras were to be placed. Brooke moved stealthily through the trees and the brush, doing her best not to make a sound. She breathed slowly, keeping herself calm so she didn't make a mistake.

As the lights to the complex became more apparent, the less beneficial her goggles became. She placed them back in her pack as she took cover behind a tree. She knew she was about fifty feet from her desired location and peered around the tree to see if there were any obstructions to consider. It had become apparent that there were no perimeter guards this far out, so Brooke made her move around one tree and to the next, until she had made it to her proverbial X on the map.

When Brooke was nine years old, her brothers had built a tree house that they had cleverly labeled as a "boys only" space. If that had been enough to deter Brooke, she wouldn't have honed a particular skill set that she was about to put to good use. She made a leap for the lowest branch, and when she caught hold, she swung her body up and maneuvered herself so that she was straddling the branch. After she found stable footing, she stood and pulled herself to the next branch. *Thanks, boys. Couldn't have done it without you.* Brooke shimmied around the trunk and pulled out her small infrared camera. Bowing's voice came through her earpiece. "A little to the left, up, right, a little down...perfect." Brooke secured the camera and then pulled out the long-distance microphone, but she couldn't get it to stay in the tree. She realized they hadn't brought the right weights to secure it. She put it back in her pack, deciding it was better not to use it rather than make too much noise trying to secure it without the proper equipment.

Jennifer was already back at the meeting point when Brooke came up beside her. She was holding her left arm and seemed to be in pain. Brooke put her hand over hers, where Jennifer was holding herself, trying to understand what happened, but she shook her head and pulled away. Since this wasn't exactly the place to have a lengthy discussion, Brooke let it go. She pointed toward the top of the hill and they took off back to base camp.

Six minutes later, the two were back up the side of the hill and walking toward the monitoring station. Tyler saw that Jennifer was holding her arm and went to her side. "What happened, Glass?"

Jennifer slowly pulled her hand away, revealing a dark stain on her shirt. "Nothing bad, just caught my arm on a tree branch."

"Pull your shirt off," Tyler said without hesitation.

Jennifer did as she was told, her breath hissing as the shirt pulled away from the wound. Her arm revealed a four-inch gash that was almost a full two inches deep.

"You need stitches."

"Well then, give them to me out here. I'm not leaving the mission."

Upon hearing that the wound needed stiches, Brooke hurried over and grabbed the first aid kit. She tried to give Jennifer a reassuring smile and started cleaning out her wound. Several pieces of fabric and some tree particles had to be removed with tweezers before the gooey mess could be stitched up, and Jennifer was doing her very best macho impression as Brooke diligently did what needed to be done. "I know this hurts. I'm sorry."

Jennifer shook her head, gritting her teeth. "Just get it cleaned out and closed up."

Brooke continued to concentrate, still acutely aware that Tyler was standing behind her watching her work.

Brooke glanced around briefly. "Everything up and running okay?" She decided to have this conversation now because it was harder to concentrate in the silence and she didn't want to give Jennifer anything more to gossip about.

"You both did a fine job," Tyler responded quietly.

Brooke liked when her voice was almost at a whisper. As always, her involuntarily response to Tyler was to feel a rush go through her body. Her face flushed, and there was nothing she could do to stop it, so she concentrated harder on keeping her hands steady as she worked the needle, stitching the thread through Jennifer's arm.

"Thanks, Brooke," Jennifer said once the final knot had been tied.

"I'm going to put a clean dressing on it, but we need to check it every few hours to make sure you don't get an infection."

Jennifer nodded and walked over to grab her canteen, looking faintly unsteady on her feet.

"She'll be fine, Brooke."

Brooke glanced over at Tyler, who looked impossibly sexy leaning against a tree, a faint light shadowing her defined arms. "I know. I just don't like to see anyone hurt, even Jennifer."

Tyler pushed herself off the tree and walked past Brooke, brushing her shoulder with her own. "She knows what her body can handle."

Brooke knew Tyler was talking about Jennifer's injury, but the feeling of Tyler being that close, and remembering how she'd been injured so recently herself, caused Brooke to shiver. *This is going to get worse before it gets better.* Brooke tried to stay focused on the mission. "Still, I'm going to bring Patrick down with us for the final portion. If this little mishap taught me anything, it's that we need a backup in case something happens to one of us. Carlson can work the computers. We won't need a watch at that point."

Carlson came down from the lookout location and Bowing took his spot. Brooke had established a watch rotation, placing herself at the coldest part of the night, zero two hundred through zero four hundred. There was a lot she wanted to get done before then, and sleep wasn't something she was interested in. The team assembled around the monitors and starting tracking the people moving around the complex via the infrared cameras they'd put in place. Brooke gave specific instructions to monitor the numbers, change of watch times, how long the transition took, and if it was a rotating post or the same people coming in and out.

She knew the people they were monitoring were another group of recruits, in their testing phase, probably with the mission of not allowing infiltration, but it didn't make them feel any less the target. She looked around at her teammates and realized that they were all feeling that surge of adrenaline; they were finally putting all their skills to use. *Except...where is Carlson?* Brooke shrugged it off. Carlson had an odd fear of urinating in front of people and probably went to find the farthest tree possible, within the perimeter. She took a quick glance at her watch. The night air was crisp, biting. It was going to be a long night, with so much that hung in the balance. There were so many things that could happen, that could go wrong. Brooke fought the urge to pinch the bridge of her nose. She didn't want to give the impression to any of her teammates that she was worried, and she never knew who was watching.

CHAPTER TEN

Tyler watched from the shadows as Brooke paced. She knew the tactic well. It was the time of morning when it was almost impossible to stay awake, and on watch, falling asleep wasn't acceptable. Moving around helped. She could see Patrick in the distance, monitoring the surveillance equipment, his head constantly dropping forward as he fought to stay awake. Carlson and Glass were sleeping. Hopefully. Everyone needed to be in perfect form when it came time to move. She started toward Brooke, though she hadn't intended to. A branch broke under her feet, and Brooke spun around, her gun in hand.

Tyler emerged from the trees with her hands up and Brooke flipped up her goggles and walked over. "You scared the shit out of me. I could have shot you!"

"Well, seeing as those bullets are rubber, I probably would have survived, and I taught you better than to shoot at an unidentified target."

Brooke punched Tyler in the arm. "You could have warned me."

"Yeah, you're right. I should have shouted your name out as I was walking through the forest. I'll do that next time."

Brooke rolled her eyes. "Always the comedian, I see. Even at the butt crack of dawn."

Tyler didn't realize she had placed her hand on Brooke's back as they spoke. She moved her hand away like she'd been burned. *Pay attention. Focus. Stop acting without thinking.*

"You don't have to take your hand off me." Brooke's vulnerability seeped through in her tone, another reminder of things she liked so much about Brooke.

"Yes, I do. I shouldn't have come over. I'm sorry. I'm going to go."

Brooke took Tyler's hand and placed it against her chest. "Don't go yet." She held Tyler's hand as they stood in front of each other, close enough Tyler could feel the rise and fall of Brooke's chest.

She closed her eyes and focused on the sound of Brooke's breathing. It was reassuring, comforting, and it felt…safe.

Brooke slowly moved her hand up Tyler's arm, and although she had long ago put on a thick black fleece, she could feel each of Brooke's fingertips with excruciating intimacy. Tyler's voice dried up and her breath hitched. *Say it. Walk away. Do something.* "I'm going to get some sleep."

"Okay." Brooke moved against Tyler's body and pressed her lips against her mouth.

Tyler hesitated for a moment. She could feel her control slipping, and as she desperately tried to hold on to the last thread of her resolve, she heard a soft moan escape the back of Brooke's throat, and her knees almost gave out. She forcibly pushed herself away. "I can't. I'm sorry, but I can't." Her breath was ragged. She was trying to control it and everything else her body was experiencing. Looking at Brooke was too painful, so she turned her back before she could say the next words. "I wish this was different, I wish *I* was different, but I'm not."

A voice coming through the mic interrupted the moment.

"Hart, come in, Hart." Brooke failed to respond, and Tyler looked over her shoulder. She was simply staring at Tyler, her eyes filled with hurt.

"Hart, is everything okay? Come in, Hart?"

Tyler whispered, "You need to answer that."

Brooke seemed to snap out of it. "Go for Hart."

"What the fuck, Brooke? Is everything okay?"

Brooke put her hand over her eyes. "Yes, sorry. Everything is fine. Perimeter clear." Even through the crackled radio transmission, Brooke could hear Patrick's irritation.

"Don't miss the next check-in."

"I won't, Bowing."

Tyler finally turned around. *Stop being a coward. Say it and walk away.* "I'm sorry."

Brooke shook her head. "No, I'm sorry. I don't know what it is about you. Getting through this curriculum has been the only thing that has mattered to me for a year. But you show up and I start to fuck it all away."

Tyler placed her hands on her hips. "You're right. I'm a terrible distraction for you, a distraction you can't afford."

Brooke held up her hands. "That's not what I meant, Tyler. You're a good distraction."

"There is no such thing, Brooke. Not in the line of work we do."

"Yes, we're going to need to make some adjustments, but this feeling, you and I, isn't something that I'm willing to walk away from, especially before it really gets started."

Tyler was getting frustrated, not with Brooke, but with herself. "Don't you see, a distraction is the difference between life and death. I put you at risk."

Brooke took a step forward. "This is a training mission. No one is trying to kill me."

"They won't always be training missions."

Brooke tried to take her hand again. "I'm not a Marine, and you're a distraction I want."

"I won't risk you. There are things you don't know. Things you don't understand." Tyler wasn't going to discuss it any further. She moved into the darkness, feeling more alone than she ever had before.

She walked down the hill, barely paying attention to her surroundings. This behavior, acting like this, wasn't something she understood or had ever done. She was a Marine and a damn good one. She wanted to protect others, fight for her country, and serve honorably. She wasn't feeling very honorable. She pulled out her phone and called Nicole.

❖

Glass came up the side of the hill at zero three forty-five to take over the watch. Brooke barely looked at her before pulling out her earpiece and storming away. She was going to find Tyler and they were going to have a conversation. She wasn't going to let Tyler push her away just because there was something she was afraid to deal with. Maybe she was scared of what they felt for each other, or scared of losing someone else, or scared she wasn't good enough. There seemed to be no end to the list of fears that Tyler might have when it came to Brooke, but she wasn't going to let her demolish their relationship before it even started. It wasn't fair, and it wasn't right.

This is the right thing to do. She's in the wrong. I can do this. She opened the army green flap on Tyler's tent to find Nicole Sable sitting with her legs crossed, reading the mission briefing report with a flashlight in her mouth. Nicole looked up from the binder and took the light from between her lips.

Brooke felt like she was seeing a ghost. Maybe that's what it was. Maybe there was someone else…

"Can I help you, Hart?"

Brooke couldn't find her voice. She stared at Nicole, willing her to change into Tyler. "Sorry, I was looking for Tyler. Sergeant, I mean."

"She wasn't feeling well. She asked me to complete the training exercise."

"Oh. Sure."

"She didn't tell me anything else, Brooke. I'm sorry."

Brooke nodded and backed away from the tent feeling like someone had just punched her in the stomach. Tyler had left them on their own, because of her. She'd taken Tyler away from the team, not just herself. She felt selfish and foolish. She went to her tent and cried herself to sleep.

Kyle put his arm around her and started guiding her up to the steps of the building. "What's off is that it's Friday night and we're sober and at work."

Tyler could see why Nicole had fallen for Kyle. He had a way of making you feel better without the macho, condescending attitude. "You're right. When this is done, drinks are on me."

"Ha! Don't make promises you can't afford to keep, Monroe. You've never seen me drink when it's free."

"Challenge accepted." She pushed into him, feeling somewhat better as they entered the building.

Together, they walked to another room, where they could watch the training exercise unfold from the confines of a claustrophobic monitoring room where the smell of day-old coffee lingered in every corner. Tyler quickly scanned all the monitors until she felt her heart rate subside. Brooke's voice was crystal clear over the radio, in contact with Carlson, who apparently was placed at the campsite to monitor the evolution. Tyler had already anticipated where Brooke would have placed her fellow classmates. She'd understood their strengths and weaknesses and harnessed each accordingly. She was proud of her.

❖

Thompson hopped out of the vehicle and went around to the trunk of the SUV. His black BDUs helped him blend into the night, and he loved the stealthy feel of it. He checked his sidearm, his earpiece, and his watch. It wouldn't be long now. Eleven men came up behind him, awaiting further instructions. They all were dressed the same way, and Thompson had a surge of power run through him. The next few hours would change his life forever. He would have power and control beyond

CHAPTER ELEVEN

Night was falling. It wouldn't be long now. The lights of the Farm came into view over the horizon, and Thompson shifted in his seat with excitement. It was sickening what easy prey his targets were. How easily people could be manipulated, bought, and persuaded into treason. The computer banks at the Farm housed hundreds of thousands of completed mission statistics and scenario breakdowns. The scenarios were used in training for the current recruits, and even though people's names had been changed, locations, informants, safe houses, and targets hadn't. Emergency protocols and evacuation plans for the executive branch were located in those systems, and if everything went according to plan, he would have the information without anyone knowing. A so-called terrorist attack would send the country into mayhem and its leaders right into his hands.

And while chaos reigned, he'd take some time to get to know Tyler Monroe. He had a special set of knives sharpened, and he planned to use every single one of them to cut through her disgusting body.

❖

The more time Brooke spent without Tyler around, the more uneasy she felt. She hated that there were things unsaid between them, and she hated that Tyler left without saying anything about where she was going. She could feel her frustration mounting, and she knew she was looking at the monitors without taking anything in.

"You really need to focus."

There was so much compassion in Patrick's eyes, so much understanding. She had been on point all day with surveillance, but Patrick knew her better than anyone and understood just how distracted she truly was. "I just…" Brooke shook her head. This wasn't the time or place for the distraction bombarding her.

He squeezed her shoulder. "We can talk about it later. Let's just get through the next twenty-four hours."

Brooke took a deep breath and nodded. Nothing ever threw her off her game, and she hated feeling so out of sorts. *Take control. Focus.*

Brooke walked over to the table with the map of their location to look over the routes she had already engraved in her memory.

Nicole walked over and stood beside her. "Have the routes changed from the last thirty times that you looked them over?" There was a hint of sympathy in her smile, and she cocked her head.

"No. I just want to make sure there are no surprises."

Nicole nodded. "Good call." Softly, she said, "She'll come around, Hart. In time."

Brooke looked at Nicole, unsure what to say. "I, um…"

"There's no need to explain. All I'm saying is, she likes you a lot, and she *will* come around. However, you need to get through this mission, and you've got to focus on the here and now. For yourself, and for your team."

Brooke swallowed the lump in her throat. "You're righ Thank you."

Brooke decided that it was time to move this testing along so she could get some answers. She called her teammates over to the table to prepare for the mission. They filed over one by one. Each looked both excited and apprehensive, and she imagined she looked the same way. Personalities aside, they were in this together, all the way to the end. She opened her notepad and started going through the plan of attack and discussing each of their roles in detail.

❖

Tyler paced up and down the steps of the monitoring building.

"You're making me crazy." Kyle poked at her, half kidding, half serious.

Tyler stopped in her tracks. "I shouldn't have left them up there."

Kyle shook his head. "It's not like they're alone. Nicole is up there. Nothing bad is going to happen. It's a training mission, for God's sake."

Tyler pushed her hand through her hair. "I know. It's just that, they're my team, and I should be up there. I shouldn't have let personal crap get in the way of a mission."

Kyle stood and placed his hands on Tyler's shoulders. His eyes were kind, and Tyler bit back the urge to hug him.

"You did what you needed to do to make sure all your students were successful and focused on the mission, including Brooke. That's more important than being up there to witnes it firsthand. Nicole can take care of the assessments."

Tyler shook her head. "I just can't shake the feeling tha something is off."

his wildest dreams. Money was a nice accessory, but it was nothing compared to power. With power, he could control the outcome of history, the way people addressed and respected him. Fortunes were won and lost over the course of a lifetime, but powerful men were written about in history books and had statues erected in their honor. The icing on the cake was that by this time tomorrow, he would have Tyler Monroe's heart on a platter.

He had spent months planning for this night, and what seemed like a lifetime dreaming of it. The only thing that stood between him and his destiny was one mile of trees and strategically placed monitoring cameras, which he had already located and would be in control of in a matter of minutes. His self-appointed computer genius would compromise the security network from inside the SUV, making their approach undetectable. It was a perfect plan. The Farm had a closed-circuit monitoring system, meaning that you had to actually be inside the facility in order to tap into the system or be able to set up a link directly into the system itself, which was exactly what they were going to do.

The Farm's main gate was monitored by guards, but the fences that surrounded the facility were sparsely guarded and penetrable. Thompson already had the locations of all of the cameras, thanks to hacking their computer system months ago. *Smartest people in the country, my ass.* The tech handed Thompson a small black box with a stubby antenna in the back. He needed to place it directly onto one of the cameras in order for the tech to hack into the monitoring system. Thompson wasn't going to leave this task up to any of the brainless morons he'd recruited for this night. As soon as it was over, they too would be eliminated. He'd enjoy doing it himself.

Thompson walked along the chain link fence until he found a spot hidden with brush and shadows. He clipped a hole in the fence just big enough to wedge his body through, approximately ten feet from the closest camera. As he got closer, he could see the blinking red light. *You would think they'd make more of an effort to disguise these things.* He made his way around the back of the post and pulled out the large leather strap he'd purchased from a lineman's shop. He put the strap around his waist and the pole and shimmied up the side. His arms and legs were shaking by the time he reached the top, but he made sure to go as slowly as possible so as to not disturb the camera. It was taxing on his patience and muscles. He pulled off the adhesive piece attached to the small black box and placed it gently on the side of the camera. He pushed the On button and waited for confirmation.

The tech's voice came in clear. "We're up and running."

Thompson shimmied back down, adrenaline and self-congratulations spurring him on. *Now things will change. I'm coming for you, Monroe.*

❖

Tyler hadn't been able to shake the unease she continued to feel, and now the panic was mounting. She scanned the surveillance cameras again, and there was nothing out of place, which was exactly how it should be. The team had purposely avoided the system's line of sight in order to evade their opponents. She turned to check the outlying cameras and noticed that post 68-A was shaking. *What the fuck?* She stepped closer to the monitor to get a better look. The monitor blinked twice and returned to normal, no shaking, no movement. The time stamp read correctly, but she knew something was off, and she wouldn't ignore the feeling again.

She thought briefly about alerting the director but decided better of it. She didn't want to seem skittish. She'd go investigate the situation on her own, to put her mind at ease. She grabbed a radio from the bank in the corner of the room and whispered in Kyle's ear, "I'm going to head up the hill for a bit, by the outlying cameras. I need to check on something." She headed outside.

Kyle quickly caught up with her. "You didn't think I was going to let you go wandering off all by yourself, did you?" He had grabbed a radio himself, along with a flashlight. He tossed her a set of keys. "You drive." He jogged over to the passenger side of the all-terrain vehicle and jumped in.

Tyler was going to protest, but the thought of someone going with her was reassuring, especially since her sixth sense was telling her something was seriously off. She jumped into the driver's seat. "Thanks, Kyle."

He nodded and they headed out into the darkness together.

❖

Thompson and his men moved through the trees with speed and agility. The bank of computers they were looking for was kept in an underground vault accessed from the main administrative building, but stupidly, an emergency access tunnel was attached to it. This tunnel was also to serve as an escape route, which would have been effective, if the location was kept unknown and wasn't about to be used for entry rather than exit.

Thompson looked up from the map when he sensed movement in the darkness ahead. *What the fuck...* He held up his hand as an indication for his men to stop. He couldn't figure out what was going on. The access tunnel was located in what was supposed to be an empty building. *Empty. It's supposed to be fucking empty.*

Far from empty, the area was lit up with patrols. He took

another step forward and heard movement in the brush. He flipped down his goggles to see a person slowly creeping forward toward the building. He crept up on her, and just as she spun to face him, he slammed his flashlight against her skull, knocking her to the ground.

Thompson's thoughts raced. *That won't be the only one.* He grabbed the earpiece out of her ear and placed it in his own.

A man's voice came over. "Hart, control." Seconds passed. "Hart, control." A few more seconds. "Glass, control."

"Go ahead, control."

"We're having some signal interference with the cameras up here. Seems Hart may be experiencing the same difficulties."

"Roger that, control."

"Hart, you copy?"

Thompson clicked the radio link several times. He hoped that whoever this girl was with would take that as her trying to communicate. There was silence over the line. *They bought it for now.* His head was reeling. Whatever was happening, whatever reason they were there, would obviously begin soon and they would notice her gone. There were too many people with him to continue to go undetected, but he wasn't going to get a chance like this again. He motioned his men back up the hill to the vehicles. He'd wait with the girl until he figured out the next step. Maybe this would play out in his favor. If these people were going to cause a distraction, he might be able to slip in and out with even greater ease.

He looked down at the woman at his feet. In the faint light he could make out the contours of her face. *Aren't you a hot little piece of ass?* He pulled her head up by the hair to get a better look and then dropped it back to the ground with a quiet thud. He pulled the radio loose from her pants and pulled her sidearm from its holster. He released the clip and inspected the bullets. He shook his head and put the gun in the back of his pants. *Fucking rubber bullets. It's a damn training mission.*

❖

Tyler and Kyle made it to post 68-A, stopped the vehicle, and hopped out.

"What exactly are we looking for?"

Tyler shook her head and wandered in circles around the tall piece of wood. "I'm not sure exactly. It was shaking on the monitor and then there was nothing." She patted her stomach. "Something just doesn't seem right, here."

Kyle pulled the flashlight from his pocket and started shining it up and down the post. He reached the top where the camera was placed and squinted. "I don't know if my eyes are playing tricks on me, but it looks like there's something attached up there."

Tyler went to the back of the vehicle and pulled out the pole climbing equipment. She proceeded to suit up and shimmied her way up the side. When she reached the top, she shined her flashlight on the camera, and her stomach tightened when she realized what was attached.

"Well?" Kyle called from the bottom.

Tyler hurried down the post. "Someone has tapped the camera system, probably to loop the surveillance."

"Part of the training mission?"

Tyler shook her head. "No, we never came up this far."

Kyle still looked perplexed. "We need to get to the control station." He looked back up at the camera. "Shouldn't we get it down?"

Tyler shook her head as she ran back to the vehicle. "No, we have the upper hand right now. We know they're here and they don't know we're on to them. It might buy us some time to figure out what the hell is going on."

Tyler and Kyle rapidly headed back to the control station. The two people watching the monitors turned quickly.

"What's wrong?"

Tyler started scanning the monitors, explaining what had just taken place, desperately looking for any sign of Brooke and the rest of the team.

"We need to call them back," Kyle said.

"No, not yet." Tyler knew she could be playing with fire, but she didn't know what was going on yet, and any deviation could put people in danger. Her people. She wasn't going to let that happen again. She radioed Carlson on a private channel. "Status?"

"We've had some interference and I can't get in touch with Hart."

Tyler's stomach hit the ground. "What do you mean?" *Calm. Focus. Don't let your team down.*

"I…we…I've talked to Glass and Bowing, but I can't get Hart to call back on the radio. Do you want me to try again?"

"No. Stand by and wait for further instructions." She looked over at Kyle. "Is her transmitter still on?"

Kyle looked down at the monitors. "Yes." He pointed to the screen where there was a reassuring blinking red light. "She's still in the correct position too. She should be there"— Kyle glanced at his watch—"for another seventeen minutes."

Tyler went to the back of the vehicle and Kyle followed. She inspected the rifle and placed it next to her.

"What should we do now?"

Tyler didn't look up as she placed a knife in a small ankle holster and attached it to her leg. "You need to get over to the main building and let the director know. We can't use the radio to communicate because if they have gotten to Brooke, they could have her radio."

Kyle handed Tyler a Kevlar vest from the back of the vehicle. "You're going after her, aren't you?"

Tyler pulled the vest over the top of her head and started to adjust the straps. "Of course I am. I would go after any of them. Whatever is going on, it may have nothing to do with them, and they could be safe as could be. But I'm not taking that chance. I'll get them out of the field, and then we'll figure out what the hell is going on." She fitted the rifle strap over the vest and glanced at Kyle.

"This isn't just any one of them though, Tyler. It's Brooke."

Tyler checked her sidearm, not bothering to respond. She needed to keep under control right now, and that meant not talking about the possibility that Brooke was in real trouble.

"Please just be careful. Your emotions are all wrapped up in this one. And emotions can get you dead."

Tyler stopped adjusting her straps and looked at him. The worry, the friendship, and the concern tore at her heart. "This is what I do. It's what I'm good at, and—"

"And you love her." Kyle finished Tyler's thought for her. He grabbed Tyler and hugged her before she had a chance to say anything else. "Be careful."

Kyle squeezed her shoulder and Tyler nodded. He climbed into another vehicle and said, "I'll go fill in the director."

"Keep one of the radios tuned in to channel twelve. I'll call you on that if there's an emergency." Tyler placed the bud into her ear, changed the frequency on the radio, and then headed down the hill. If Brooke was in position and her radio was simply bad, it was an easy fix and Tyler could focus on the other issue at hand. If she wasn't there…Tyler swallowed back bile. *Fuck.*

CHAPTER TWELVE

B rooke's head felt like it was about to split wide open. A wave of nausea washed over her, and she coughed. Before she could get her hand to the back of her head where the shooting pain was originating from, a hand grabbed her throat, pulled her onto her feet, and slammed her against a tree. The grip was so tight Brooke felt like she was underwater, unable to reach the top. Hot, stale breath whispered in her ear.

"Make a fucking sound and I'll end you."

Brooke couldn't respond, and she was clawing at the hand threatening to send her into the darkness once again. Air rushed into her lungs, and she gasped, feeling like she'd never been allowed to breathe before. She knew by the lightness on her hip that her gun had been removed, so she didn't bother to reach for it to make sure, knowing that the motion could send her attacker back into a rage. "Who are you?" Her voice cracked, and her hand went up to her neck in an unconscious soothing motion, but the pain wasn't going to abate.

"What's important is what I am, not who I am. And right now, I'm the person who has decided not to kill you. For the moment."

Brooke knew he was telling the truth, though she could hear the hatred in his voice.

"You're going to help me finish what I need to do. If you cooperate, I won't kill you."

She couldn't make out his face clearly in the blackness, but she didn't need to. She instinctively knew he was lying. It didn't matter what she did; he was going to kill her either way. Buying time in order to create an opportunity to escape was the only option she had.

He put his hand up to his ear, listening.

The darkness can be your ally or your enemy. Brooke was thankful for Tyler's words, because it helped shield her emotions, which were rapidly transcending from fear into anger. This wasn't part of their training mission; she knew that much. The anger and rage emanating from the man couldn't be faked. He was here for an entirely different purpose, and that thought alone shook her to the core. "What exactly are you trying to do?" She had said it just above a whisper because he was close enough she knew he would hear it. She needed to figure him out, quickly—his strengths and weaknesses, both physically and mentally. She could feel his head shift toward her and saw an evil smile twist his mouth.

"I'm taking my rightful place in history." He turned back toward the compound.

Great, he really is a fucking whacko. "They're going to realize I'm not with them, you know." She knew she was pushing it, but she wanted to test his patience to see exactly what the parameters were.

He shrugged. "Ha! This is a training mission. You're all a bunch of amateurs. They aren't going to notice anything before it is too late. They'll just think you've done something stupid and tell you off for it later. I could always drag your pretty ass back up the hill. Let all my men have their way with you. But if you don't shut up, I'm going to slit your throat and leave you out here to die."

"My sergeant will know."

He grabbed her throat again and placed his lips against her cheek. "I do hope so. I'm going to fucking gut Monroe from belly to throat." He licked the side of her face and pushed her backward.

Chills rippled through Brooke's body at the reference to Tyler. She tried to work through her training and stay focused on the little bit of information that she'd been able to obtain. "How do you know the sergeant?"

"What?" he said, his tone frustrated.

"You mentioned her by name. How do you know the sergeant?"

He pushed his gun up under her chin, forcing her head back into the tree. "You talk too fucking much."

❖

Tyler had made it to the blinking red dot on her handheld monitor in record time and was watching the interaction from a distance. She forced her body to stay in one place as she watched the gun get shoved into Brooke's throat. She couldn't hear what they were saying, but she didn't need to. The fact that he touched Brooke at all was a good enough reason to kill him. She took the rifle off her back and started to adjust the scope. *Stop. Think.*

The man didn't deserve to take another breath, but she needed information from him before she ended his miserable existence. She cussed at herself as she slung the rifle back over her shoulder. She needed to see where he was going, what he was doing, and who exactly he was working for. It took balls to break into a CIA facility, balls she would gladly remove once they finally met face-to-face. *Stay strong, Brooke. I'm here.*

She listened to her radio, taking into account where the other recruits were with regard to the mission. Whatever the hell was going on, they could be in danger too, and she'd be damned if she was going to let anyone get hurt. Glass checked in quietly. She'd made it into the compound right on time. Tyler could picture her as she maneuvered through dark corners and hid behind a large set of metal containers, as was often the case with this particular training mission. Patrols often got lazy and complacent, since they hadn't been told when the mission would take place, as a way to train those agents too. She said she was in position and waiting.

Patrick was the next to check in, and Tyler could hear his voice getting frantic. "Control, Bowing."

Chris's voice came over the line. "Go ahead, Bowing."

"Hart's transmitter is in the same location. Is there an update on her status?"

Thankfully, the next voice to come on the line was Kyle's. "Seems to be a radio malfunction, Bowing. Stay in position."

❖

Thompson had pressed the radio into his ear as he listened in on the conversation going on with the woman's team. Once again, he grabbed Brooke by the throat. "I'm losing my patience with you."

His breath reeked of stale potato chips and soda, and it made Brooke's stomach turn as bits of spit clung to the side of his face as he talked.

"I don't know what you're talking about," she managed to choke out before his grip tightened again.

"You have a fucking tracking device on you, you stupid bitch."

His anger was clearly growing with each passing second,

and Brooke wasn't sure how much longer he would hold out before snapping her neck. He seemed like the type of person who threw temper tantrums when he didn't get his way. "I thought you had found it. I wasn't trying to deceive you. If you give me the radio, I will check in and no one will be the wiser."

Thompson seemed to ponder that possibility for a moment, and Brooke thought he might actually believe her. There was a shift in the night air, clearing his awful stench for a moment, and Brooke glanced over his shoulder. Thompson caught her eye movement and pulled her around into his chest, gun pressed into her temple, the force causing a silver flash of pain through her skull.

"I'll put a bullet in her head." He growled out into the nothingness, searching the darkness for an enemy.

Tyler took a step forward, her gun aimed at Thompson's head. "Let her go."

Thompson laughed. It was a nasty, sadistic sound. "Fuck you, Monroe."

If Tyler was surprised he knew her name, she didn't show it. "Let her go and you can have me instead."

Brooke pulled at the arm around her neck. "No! No, Tyler!"

He flashed a smile at Tyler. "Put your weapons on the ground, all of them."

Tyler pulled her rifle off her back and placed it on the ground, still keeping her 9mm Beretta pointed at Thompson's face. "Let her go and I'll put the gun down."

Thompson pulled harder on Brooke's neck and pushed more forcefully with his gun. Either the front sight or the muzzle of the gun had apparently penetrated her skin, and she felt blood seep slowly down the side of her face. She let tears fall, but didn't give out a single whimper or acknowledgment of the pain. She wouldn't give him the satisfaction. Tyler motioned with both hands in the air and placed the gun on the ground.

Fear shattered Brooke's composure. "Tyler, no! He'll kill you. He already said he would."

Keeping his eyes fixed on Tyler, Thompson forcefully kissed the side of Brooke's face and shoved her away, causing her to stumble.

Brooke wanted to run to Tyler, to block the threat, but Tyler held up her hand to stop her, while keeping her eye on their assailant. She knelt, dizzy, her head spinning, and tried desperately to follow the situation, begging her body to do what she needed it to.

Thompson was immediately on top of Tyler, forcing her to her knees with his gun thrust against her forehead.

"You don't want to do that." Tyler's voice was so calm, so composed, Brooke momentarily thought she might be slipping into shock.

"I'll do whatever I want, to whomever I want, Monroe."

"You're obviously a smart man. You managed to break into this facility, undetected, and with quite a bit of ease. You had a reason for coming here, and it wasn't for Recruit Hart. You wanted something, and I can help you get it."

Thompson's eyes seemed to match the black of the sky, void of empathy or emotion. He waited for Tyler to continue.

"If you kill me, you're giving them the opportunity to catch you."

This seemed to snap Thompson back into reality and his task at hand. He took a half step backward. "One wrong move, and I won't shoot you. I'll fillet you and piss on the remains."

Tyler nodded in acknowledgment. She threw Brooke a look, as though to warn her from making a move.

There could be no mistakes.

❖

This was the cherry on top of the cake for Thompson. Emotional pain was far more poignant than physical. Physical wounds healed, emotional wounds oozed right below the surface for a lifetime. And he knew just how Tyler would feel, watching him handle one of her little soldiers. Thompson pulled a cell phone out of his pocket and flipped it open, keeping the gun trained on Tyler. "Stay in position until I call you again. There's been a change in plans." He closed the phone and slipped it back into his pocket. He was pleased with himself. He took his time holstering his gun. Things weren't going as planned, but it could be they'd gone even better than he'd hoped.

Thompson pulled the eight-inch hunting knife from a holster near his boot, flipping it over in his hand a few times, then he pulled the tip of it down Tyler's cheek. The scraping sound of the tip to Tyler's skin was the most painful thing that Brooke had ever felt.

"Leave us. I have my hostage. Do anything stupid and she dies. And it won't be a nice, clean death, either." His expression as he stared at Tyler was creepy, obsessed.

Brooke didn't respond. If she left, she could get help. If she left, he could kill Tyler and escape. If she stayed, she couldn't get help, and both of them might die. Neither of them could outrun a bullet.

"You're really starting to irritate me." He pressed the knife deeper into Tyler's cheek and was rewarded with a soft hiss.

"Okay, please, just don't hurt her."

He ran his finger over the blood and then licked it from his finger. "Oh, it's going to hurt as I taste every part of her." He grabbed between Tyler's legs and squeezed her crotch. "Going to hurt so much, you'll be begging for death. But you, little soldier, can't do anything about it. Leave or I'll kill you now."

Tyler spoke softly. "Get out of here, Brooke."

Brooke wanted to tell her no, that she wouldn't leave her and that they could kick this pervert's ass.

"Now, Brooke! That's an order," Tyler said more forcibly this time.

Her heart was screaming to stay with Tyler, but her head wanted to listen to her instructor, a Marine that knew more about this type of situation than she felt ready to evaluate. Without saying another word, Brooke took off running toward the top of the hill.

"Alone at last." He yanked Tyler up by her arm and pointed her body in the direction of the compound. "Take off that vest. If I want to shoot you, I don't need any interference. Not that I couldn't just shoot you between the eyes. But that wouldn't take long enough."

Tyler obliged, loathing that every movement could be sealing her fate, but also aware that every moment they remained in place gave Brooke more time to get backup.

"Put your hands behind your head. Take me there." He motioned toward the compound.

Tyler moved in the appointed direction, glad he hadn't actually tied her hands in any way. She stayed slightly to his left, wanting to keep him in her peripheral vision, and he didn't correct the position, which told her he was an amateur. If she could get a bit of room, just a few feet so she could spin and kick... "If you tell me what you're looking for, I could probably save you a lot of time."

He gave a long, irritated sigh, followed by a muffled pop from what she knew instinctively was a silencer, before she felt a searing pain in her right thigh. She fell to the ground holding her leg and gasping for air. She didn't have to see the wound to know she had been shot. The immediate sensation of a drill being taken to your body was unmistakable. She said between labored breaths, "You could have just said you didn't want to tell me."

"That wasn't for the question. That was because I've wanted to shoot you for months. Besides, we're just getting started. There's plenty of time." He pulled Tyler to her feet by her hair, and she struggled not to let the pain show.

Tyler limped forward, the pain excruciating, but she forced her mind and body to push through. The adrenaline was a powerful mask for what she was enduring, but if he'd hit her femoral artery, she'd be dead in two minutes, maybe three. Given that she was still moving, he must have missed it. Tyler forced herself toward the well-lit compound. *What the hell is he thinking, taking me toward people who can help me?* This wouldn't end well for the recruits on the other side of the fence who were protected by nothing except a few rounds of rubber bullets in their guns. "You don't want to go over there. Take me someplace out of the compound and we can talk. I can help you get what you want. You just need to tell me what it is."

One of the roving guards was making his way along the fence line. Thompson pulled out the rifle Tyler had been carrying and took aim.

"He's just a kid!" Tyler was hoping she'd said it loud enough to at least throw the rover off, even if she paid a price for it.

He exploded with rage, and there was another searing pain, this time in her side. As he pulled the wide knife blade out, she fell to the ground, gasping. Combined with the pain in her thigh, she knew she had moments before she lost consciousness. The eerie silence that had encased her after she had awakened from the roadside bomb in Iraq surrounded her again, and the man standing over her was standing near the bodies of her team splayed around her. She blinked furiously, trying to dispel the mingled scenes, knowing she needed to stay in the moment. But as the scent of blood started to choke her, the pain in her body searing through her as it did that day, she couldn't get any words out and began the slow, dizzying slide into unconsciousness.

He looked down at Tyler and spat. "I'm not going to kill you right now, Monroe. I'm going to let you bleed out. I'm going to let you die the way my brother died. The way you allowed that to happen. You killed him. Not a bomb, not any so-called terrorist, you. You stole dozens of years from my mother. Years she can never get back. Moments that she will never have with my brother. He was ten times the Marine that you are. It should have been you that day. His life was worth a dozen of yours. You're a disgrace. A pathetic placeholder for true patriotism and an embarrassment for everything real Americans value. This is your reckoning for Lance Corporal Brown."

Tyler was desperately trying to put the pieces together. Pictures of faces, memories were swimming through her mind. This was her penance, her atonement for her team's death, and it was the devil himself handing out punishment tonight.

The darkness was starting to consume her, and she struggled to stay conscious for just a little longer. She reached for the knife she kept hidden in her boot, but bending and trying to grab at the weapon sent shocks of pain deeper into her body. When she finally felt the handle, she pulled it from its holster and tried to focus on the person walking away from her.

In a final, nearly blind attempt, she hurled the knife toward the fading image.

And then the darkness claimed her.

❖

The floodlights from the compound may as well have been the sun, they were so blinding once they were activated. Thompson stumbled behind a tree, needing the protection from being seen and also to buy himself a few minutes to dislodge the knife from the back of his leg.

Useless bitch.

Tyler's loud declaration about the rover's age seemed to spur the compound to high alert. Thompson hoped they still thought they were in the midst of a training mission and went about their business accordingly. He fought the urge to pound his fists against his head, furious that he allowed his temper to get the best of him. He had bigger plans for Monroe. Plans that had her laid out on a table for hours with nothing but her own pain and regret, urged on by his blade.

He looked around desperately. He needed an escape route, and fast. His plan had gone off the rails and he needed to regroup, see if he could salvage anything. All his careful planning, all the tests he'd run and possible scenarios, had never accounted for Monroe throwing everything to shit. She'd ruined his brother's life, and now she was about to ruin his. He briefly considered turning back to finish her, to hear her scream one last time. He squinted against a brief flash in the trees, and it only took a moment to realize that the flash was, in fact, a scope.

❖

Brooke cleared the last ledge from the climb back up the hill, her heart pounding, her head throbbing. She needed to see the monitors, to get visual confirmation that Tyler was okay. *She has to be okay. She has to be. Please, God.*

Brooke made it back to the base camp they had set up over the hill. She was relieved to see Carlson's face. "What the fuck happened down there?" Carlson looked at Brooke, his worry etched on his face.

Footsteps were coming from behind. Brooke grabbed for Carlson's gun that was resting on his side. "The monitoring system should be back up and running momentarily." The sound of the director's voice offered a slight relief. He knew what was going on and he would be able to help. The director motioned for Brooke to answer the question he had apparently heard Carlson pose.

Brooke told everyone what she had just endured while frantically searching the unchanging monitors.

"I don't understand why we haven't closed in on this asshole and taken him out." Nicole pointed at Tyler's tracking device, which had moved from where they had started, but not far.

"Sergeant Monroe made the call. If he doesn't know we're on to him, we may be able to get information we need out of him. Information we can't get from the men he brought with him, and we need him alive for that. We found a dozen men scattered around the fences, camouflaged, and with enough computer equipment to shut down NASA. But they don't seem to know much beyond what their exact duties were in a given time frame. We don't know the end game yet."

The disappointment in his voice was clear, and his jaw clenched as he watched the monitors. "She warned me, you know. I blew it off as a remnant of her experience in Iraq when we didn't find anything after a full sweep, but she warned me."

Brooke shook her head. "He let me go. He has to know I would tell someone. And why aren't they moving anymore?"

Director Broadus crossed his arms over his chest. "He's assuming that he'll be finished with his task before you're able to stop him, plus he's monitoring the radio transmissions, so he thinks he'll hear us coming that way."

Brooke wasn't convinced. "He *knew* Sergeant Monroe, and I think running into her has thrown him off his game and original plan. That means we don't know what he's going to do next. We have to go to them." The monitors blinked three times and changed to the original feeds. The floodlights to the compound were in full security alert. Brooke leaned in closer. "That's not right."

They scanned through the different camera channels, trying to find a better angle of the surrounding area. Suddenly, they saw what they were looking for.

Tyler's body lay perfectly still in the bottom right monitor, a dark pool surrounding her. She was alone.

"No." Brooke wasn't sure if she had said it or thought it, but it didn't matter. Her heart splintered into tiny shards of glass and dropped into the pit of her stomach. Broadus pushed a few buttons on his phone and spoke too quietly for any of them to hear. He said he'd be back in contact soon and was gone.

Or maybe he wasn't. It was all taking shape like a nightmare she couldn't wake up from, no matter how hard she tried or how awful it became.

"I'm going to go get her." Brooke wasn't seeking anyone's approval. She said it out loud, almost to herself, in an effort to get some focus and as a way to derail the sense that her body wasn't up to the task.

Nicole was by her side instantly, handing her a radio. "I'm going with you." She threw open the metal chest and grabbed a gun for herself and handed one to Brooke.

Brooke didn't bother arguing. There would have been no point. Both took off in a full run down the side of the hill again. Just as they passed the first embankment, the loud blaring of sirens filled the air.

CHAPTER THIRTEEN

As soon as the sirens began piercing through the speakers rigged throughout the facility, Thompson ran from Monroe's body, figuring he'd better get well away from her if she was wearing a tracker. He moved behind a tree and pulled the rifle from his back. The radio in his ear started spewing instructions, describing his possible location and that he was armed and dangerous. He smiled to himself. *You have no idea.* If he was going down, he was taking as many people as he could with him. He shot toward the branches where he thought the scope was coming from, but nothing fell from the tree, so he shot again. Still, nothing.

Thompson watched the tree shiver. A shadowed figure was sliding down and he took aim again. He took his shot, but there was no indication of a direct hit. The body hit the ground and started running toward him, and then darted behind another tree when Thompson fired off another shot. Thompson shuffled to the side, dropped the rifle to his back, and grabbed his sidearm. In those brief seconds, the shadowed figure launched at him and tackled him to the ground. The first punch to the kidney made Thompson wince in pain, and the second blurred his vision as he tried to get hold of his senses. He grabbed the person and rolled over on top of him, delivering a punch hard enough he felt the man's nose break. Another hard punch to the head and the man stopped struggling. Thompson staggered off him and scanned the ground, searching for his gun, when he heard the broken pleas for help through his earpiece. It was the man lying three feet from him.

"Need…help."

Once again, his rage took over, and he jumped back on top of him when another female voice came over the radio. "I have your location, Bowing. I'm on my way."

Then another familiar voice said, "We're coming."

Thompson landed another punch to the man's face. *I should have killed that bitch when I had the chance. I wanted Monroe and I made a fucking mistake.*

Thompson kneed him in the groin and pushed him over. Thompson leveled the rifle at him, but out of the corner of his eye, another figure grabbed the 9mm he had been searching for from the ground and aimed it at him.

"Get off him."

Thompson glanced back at the woman. "Only after I kill him." He sighted down the rifle, wanting to watch the bullet go through the man's head. She wouldn't take the chance of shooting him when he was this close to his target, surely. And then he'd take her out next.

A shot echoed, but he hadn't pulled the trigger. He was puzzled for the split second before pain ricocheted through his back. He hit the ground and rolled to his side, cradling his shoulder. He could feel the saliva pooling at the corners of his mouth. The smell of sweat, blood, and hatred filled his senses. "You dumb fucking bitch! I'm going to fucking kill you!"

She walked over and kicked his gun away, keeping the gun trained at his head as she called in their location over the radio.

❖

When they finally reached Tyler, the world around Brooke became muted, as though she were underwater. She couldn't make out the siren or Nicole's voice, though she knew Nicole was calling for medics and saying the assailant was still at large. All she could see was Tyler and the blood soaking through her shirt and pants.

Brooke pulled Tyler's body close to her own. She put her hand over the wound in her side and applied as much pressure as she could manage. "Please, baby, please don't leave me. I need you. I just found you. You can't leave me."

Tyler's eyes fluttered as she clearly tried to focus. She opened her mouth as though to speak, but nothing came out.

"Hang on for me, Tyler, please."

Blood quickly covered Brooke's hands, and she'd never felt as helpless. "Oh God, Tyler, I love you. Do you hear me? I love you. Don't you dare leave me." Her tears fell and made tracks in the dirt on Tyler's face. Nicole joined her and put pressure on the leg wound. As they tried to hold Tyler's blood inside her, Brooke felt her own desperation draining her. *Please. Please, God, no. Don't take her.*

The medics arrived and hurriedly pushed Brooke and Nicole aside as they put Tyler onto the backboard and carried her up the hill through the trees, all the while checking her vitals and keeping pressure on her wounds. Brooke knew the others were following, but her entire focus was on Tyler. *So pale. Please open your eyes. Please.*

"I have a faint pulse with severe bleeding," a medic yelled to someone in the ambulance. "Run code four." They placed an oxygen mask on her and went to slam the vehicle doors shut.

"I want to go with her!" Brooke grabbed the door to stop it from closing.

"No, no one rides. Director's orders."

The medic pushed Brooke's hand away and closed the door. Nicole's arm came around Brooke's shoulder. "We'll go meet her at the hospital."

Brooke's body tensed with anger. "I want to find that fucker first." The sound of a single gunshot sent them both into a crouch on the ground. They listened and watched before moving cautiously toward the sound of the gunshot, as did the rest of the team now in place around them.

Soon, Brooke could see Jennifer standing over someone, holding them at gunpoint. Patrick was sitting on the ground, holding his nose.

Nicole looked at Brooke, still short of breath from their sprint. "Is that him?"

Brooke was seething. "Yes."

Jennifer looked back and forth between Nicole and Brooke. "Who the hell is this guy? And what the hell is going on?"

Brooke pulled the gun from Jennifer's hand. She leaned down and pushed the barrel into Thompson's forehead. "This piece of shit tried to kill Tyler."

"What? On a training mission?"

"Tried? No, I killed Monroe." Thompson stared at Brooke over the gun, not flinching.

Brooke gave him a half grin and shoved the barrel harder against his head. "No. You didn't." The look of rage that engulfed his face brought Brooke a sense of satisfaction she was sure wasn't healthy.

"You're a fucking liar!" Thompson roared.

Twenty-five armed men circled them, and Nicole ordered Brooke to drop her sidearm.

"We deal with this properly, Brooke. Stand down. Now."

She placed the gun on the ground and stepped back.

Jennifer also lowered her weapon. "We're the good guys. We're on your side," she said to the men surrounding them, weapons ready.

The director came up behind the group. "These four aren't a threat." The men changed their aim toward Thompson while the director continued to speak. "Bowing, Hart, go get some medical attention." He pointed to one of the armed men. "Take them to the hospital."

Glass threw up her hands. "Is someone going to tell me what the hell is going on?"

Nicole motioned toward the camp. "Come on. I'll fill you in."

While Nicole was walking away with Glass, Director Broadus called out, "We aren't sure the threat has been isolated. I may need you back at the main building within the hour."

He turned to Brooke and Patrick. "That goes for the two of you. Once you're done at the hospital, get back to the main building."

Brooke nodded. "Yes, sir. Permission to do one more thing?"

He nodded. "Be quick."

Brooke turned to Thompson, drew her leg back, and kicked him so solidly in the stomach she shoved him backward several inches. "That's for Tyler." He swore at her and she did it once more. "And you failed in whatever the fuck it was you were trying to do, you dirt bag." She went for one more kick, but the director put a hand on her shoulder.

"Enough. Go."

She took Patrick's arm, and they followed the agent back to camp. She felt marginally better, but worry about Tyler was tearing her apart inside. *Please. Please hold on, baby.*

Once in the car, the sudden silence and normalcy of it was surreal.

Patrick finally broke the silence. "What happened out there?"

"We'll cover it in the briefing. I don't want to talk about it right now." Brooke leaned her head back and closed her eyes. The pounding had intensified now that the adrenaline was gone, and her face hurt something fierce.

Patrick shook his head and winced at the pain. "Brooke, you have a welt on your head in the shape of a pistol barrel, cuts all over your face and body, and you just said that guy back there tried to kill the sergeant. So no, I don't want to wait for the briefing, and I don't care if you don't want to talk about it."

Brooke's eyes began to swell with tears. "I don't know if she's still alive. I don't know what's going on at all. The only thing I know is that she traded places with me. She's the reason I only have a bump on my head, and she may not make it through the night. There was so much blood, Patrick." She looked down at her hands, covered in Tyler's blood.

Patrick pulled her into an embrace. "Whatever happened, it isn't your fault. It's because of that guy back there that the sergeant is lying in a hospital bed, not you."

Brooke sobbed into his chest. "I can't lose her, Patrick."

When the car stopped in front of the military hospital, Brooke winced at the sight of Patrick's quickly bruising face. "Your poor nose."

He shrugged. "It's nothing. Get out of here. Go check on her."

"Thank you, Patrick, for everything."

He gave her a sad smile. "You don't need to thank me for being your friend, Brooke."

She kissed his cheek. "No, but I want to anyway." She helped him out of the truck. His eyes were swollen, and she could tell he was having trouble seeing where he was walking. Their driver came around and took his arm.

"I'll take him in. Check on the sarge."

Brooke gave him a grateful smile and hurried inside. She went to the nurse's station. "I need to see about Gunnery Sergeant Tyler Monroe."

The nurse didn't look up from her computer. "Are you family?"

"No, I'm her…well…her girlfriend, and I need to see her right now." Brooke knew the statement wasn't accurate but also knew it might be the only way to get information.

The nurse finally looked up, and said, "You need to get your face looked at. And I'm not letting you walk around here with blood all over your hands like some walking infection risk." She turned back to her computer screen. "I'm going to have someone come get you."

"No!" Brooke slapped her hand on the counter, heedless of the bloody handprint she left on the pristine counter. "I need to know how she is doing!"

The nurse leaned toward Brooke, unfazed. "Look, honey, I'm not going to stop you from seeing her if the doctor says it's okay, but you need attention too. You aren't going to be any good to anyone if that pretty little head of yours has a concussion. Now, go sit down." She gestured to the rows of chairs pushed up against the barren walls.

Brooke looked at the chairs, feeling like sitting there, waiting, was somehow giving up on Tyler. "Can you please just check and see if there's an update? I just need to know she's alive. Alive, that's all."

The nurse glanced up again, raising an eyebrow.

"Please, I promise I'll sit down and behave, if you can just check."

The nurse shook her head and pushed her chair out from behind the desk. She pointed at the row of chairs. "Go. Sit."

Patrick checked in and was quickly taken away, probably for X-rays. Part of her wished they'd made him come sit down too, so she'd have someone to talk to. Or even just wait with.

She was unconsciously tapping her leg up and down, earning herself an annoyed look from the elderly gentleman seated a few chairs away. She ignored him.

The double doors swung open and a doctor came out. He walked over to Brooke and sat at the table in front of her. "I'd like to have a look at your injuries. The director of your facility has personally requested me to do so, and I am being told that you're refusing care."

Brooke leaned back in her chair, growing more irritated. "I am not refusing. I said I would get looked at, but I want to know the status of Gunnery Sergeant Monroe."

"I'll give you some information. Please just come with me back into one of the examination rooms."

Brooke decided it was her only option. She pushed herself out of the chair, fighting off a wave of dizziness, and followed the doctor through the double doors and into a small room. She sat on top of the gurney and watched as he pulled a small light out of his pocket. He placed one hand on her forehead and flicked the light back and forth in her eyes. After a few moments, he started scribbling on a metal clipboard. "You have a mild concussion." He looked down at her hands, encrusted with dry blood. "Can I assume that hasn't come from you?"

Brooke fought the urge to roll her eyes. "I feel fine. And no, it's not mine. It's the sergeant's, and that's why I want to know what's going on with her."

He stopped writing and looked up at her. "You need to take this seriously. Someone needs to wake you up every few hours tonight, and if your dizzy spells get worse, I'm going to need to do a CT scan."

Brooke was going to protest about the dizziness, but before she had the chance, he held up his hand to stop her. "I saw you grab the chair out there, so don't bother with your objection."

Brooke understood that he was doing his job, that her anger and frustration was displaced. So she nodded and backed down. "I will. I promise. Now can you please tell me about the sergeant?"

He finished writing and put the chart down. "I can't give you specific information regarding her status, since you aren't family." He put his hand to the side of her face, inspecting the deep bruise.

Brooke let him inspect her. "Have you notified her family?"

"Yes, her aunt is on her way. I can tell you that she's going in for surgery right now. I'll try and give you at least a basic update when she's out of surgery."

Brooke kept her eyes focused on the ground and nodded in understanding. She didn't trust herself not to rail at him, to shake him and make him take her to Tyler.

He got up, grabbed the chart, and walked to the door. "You're welcome to wait for her family. But wash your hands first, please." He motioned at the sink. "Not only is it a health hazard, but it will scare the hell out of other people in the waiting room."

He left, and she moved numbly to the sink. As she watched Tyler's blood flow from her hands and down the drain, the anger and frustration were replaced with despair and fear. When the water finally cleared, she slid down to the floor and cried.

❖

Seconds, minutes, hours, it didn't matter. They melted together while waiting in a hospital. Patrick came out. His nose was covered in gauze bandages, and his eyes were almost swollen shut. He sat next to her and patted her leg.

"How are you feeling?" she asked.

Patrick gently touched the gauze pads. "Like I broke my nose. How about you? Have you heard anything?"

Brooke was looking at her hands, blood still encrusted around her fingernails. "Just a concussion." She paused, trying to keep her tears at bay. "I need to know she's okay."

Patrick took her hand but didn't say anything. There was nothing to say. He sat back in his seat and closed his eyes.

Nicole and Kyle came rushing through the front doors and came over to Brooke. "Any news?"

Brooke hugged them both, grateful for the company. "No, but she's been in surgery for almost three hours. The hospital notified her aunt and she should be on her way."

Nicole continued to pace, biting her nails. Kyle sat next to Patrick and started a muffled conversation that Brooke couldn't make out.

"What's going on back at the Farm?" Brooke needed something to keep her mind off of Tyler, and Nicole, who seemed grateful for the distraction, answered.

"We have a total of twelve men in custody, including the prick that tried to kill Tyler. Homeland Security is on their way down now to begin questioning. Aside from that, we still don't know what they were after."

A woman came in and rushed up to the nurses' station. There was no question about her being Tyler's aunt. The resemblance was remarkable. The blond hair and lean athletic build were clearly a blessing that the women in the family had received. When she turned around, searching the waiting area, the blue eyes shot straight to Brooke's heart.

She came over and Brooke stood up. She put out her hand to introduce herself, but the woman ignored her hand and wrapped her in an embrace. "You must be Brooke. Tyler described you perfectly."

If there was a shred of doubt she was in love with Tyler, it was shattered with that sentence. Tyler had talked about her with the only truly important person in her life, and that meant something.

"I'm Claire, Tyler's aunt."

Brooke held on tight, feeling as if this woman was keeping her from drowning. "It's so nice to meet you." Brooke quickly introduced Claire to everyone else and sat back down. Claire never let go of Brooke's hand, seeming to need an anchor as much as Brooke did.

What seemed like an eternity later, the doctor came in, his surgical mask around his neck. He smiled, and the relief Brooke felt almost buckled her knees.

"Tyler is out of surgery and doing well. She's lucky. The stab wound missed the left kidney and nicked the spleen, which we were able to repair. However, she lost a tremendous amount of blood and required a transfusion. The leg was a clean through and through and should heal nicely, although she won't have full use of her leg for several weeks."

Claire took a deep breath. "Can we please go see her?"

The doctor tilted his head. "She isn't awake, but you may go sit with her if you would like."

Claire placed her hand on Brooke's back. "Thank you."

As they walked in, Claire covered her mouth with her hand and tears ran down her cheeks.

Cuts and bruises littered Tyler's normally perfect skin, but at that moment, Brooke knew she had never seen anyone more beautiful. Brooke stood back as she watched Claire rush to Tyler's side, wipe the hair from her closed eyes, and kiss her forehead. She took her hand, seemingly mesmerized by Tyler's face. "When my sister died, it was the best, and very worst, day of my life up until then." She glanced up at Brooke and gave her a sad smile. "She has never been scared of anything, this one. My husband used to tease that she wouldn't back down from a fight with the pope if she thought she was right."

Brooke pictured Tyler as a little girl, full of vigor and courage.

Claire continued to stroke Tyler's hair. "I was so scared when she told me that she had changed her mind about the military, that she no longer wanted to be a lawyer. The idea of possibly losing her to the same people that took my Adam…it took me a long time to come to grips with it."

Brooke walked up and put a hand on Claire's back. "What made you change your mind?"

"I'm not sure I ever did, but I know that if I had to pick anyone fighting for our side, it would be Tyler."

Brooke knew exactly what Claire meant. She felt the same way about her father and brothers.

Claire walked to the door. "I need to call my neighbor. I left in such a hurry I didn't see if anyone could look after my dog. Please stay with her until I get back?"

Brooke took Claire's spot on the bed. "I'm not going anywhere," she said emphatically.

Claire smiled. "I believe that."

Brooke studied every exposed inch of Tyler. Her neck was always sleek and alluring, but all she could focus on at the moment was that there was a visible pulse, and that made it more beautiful than ever. Her arms were defined, with perfectly sculpted muscles that led to long, beautiful fingers. "I have never met anyone like you, Tyler Monroe." Brooke had to say the words, even if she didn't receive a response. "I'll never be able to thank you enough for saving my life out there, but I would like to try to make it up to you, for as long as you'll allow me to." Tyler's hand twitched under Brooke's thumb, and Brooke picked it up and kissed her knuckles. "We've only been on one real date, and I know that I love you. I can feel it in every part of my body and with every single breath that I take. I love you, Tyler." Brooke leaned down and kissed Tyler as softly as she could.

❖

Tyler wanted to force her eyes open. She needed to be awake. She needed to make sure Brooke was okay, and that the rest of the recruits were safe. She willed her eyelids to move, but they felt like they were made of lead. Her thirst was almost overwhelming, and her limbs felt like concrete.

Someone whispered in her ear. "I love you, Tyler. Wake up, baby. Please wake up."

Brooke.

She felt a hand on top of her own and lips against her forehead. She struggled to remember what had happened. Slivers of the night came rushing back to her. *Not again, please not again.*

Then another voice said softly, "Sweetheart, Brooke and I are here."

Aunt Claire. Am I dead?

"Tyler, honey, open your eyes."

The barest bits of light were starting to penetrate her eyes, and she managed a single hoarse word. "Water."

A straw touched her lips, and Tyler pulled the lukewarm fluid into her mouth. She got her eyes fully open, and the images of the two people sitting on either side of her bed started to come into focus. She saw Brooke first, and her heart flooded with relief and love.

Brooke smiled deeply at Tyler, with the one dimple that Tyler loved so much. She pulled her eyes away from Brooke and looked at her aunt.

"Oh, sweetheart, I'm so glad you're okay."

Tyler wanted to talk, wanted to tell her aunt how happy she was to see her and tell Brooke that she loved her, but she couldn't get a single word out. Exhausted, she slipped back into unconsciousness.

She heard voices in and out of her room the remainder of the day. Her aunt, a changing lineup of doctors and nurses, Nicole, Kyle, and a few more she couldn't place. The one constant voice was Brooke's, and her reassuring whispers and declarations of love. Tyler was certain that even if this was death, she didn't want anything else. What seemed like days later, she looked at the LED clock on the wall and it read 2:14 a.m. Brooke was asleep sitting next to Tyler's bed with her head resting on Tyler's hand. Tyler gently moved it so she could stroke Brooke's hair.

Brooke woke and met Tyler's eyes. The light coming from the seemingly ever-busy nurses' station outside allowed Tyler to see Brooke for the first time in what felt like years. Fatigue and pain were like makeup around Brooke's beautiful eyes. Then relief flashed over her face, and she kissed Tyler on the lips. When Tyler began to cough, Brooke quickly reached for the water, and Tyler took it from her hand, wanting to gauge how much mobility she had. She drank for several seconds and then leaned back, that simple act exhausting.

Brooke whispered, "Don't you ever scare me like that again, Monroe."

"I couldn't let him hurt you. I wouldn't have been able to live with myself if anything happened to you. I love you."

Brooke kissed her again, more slowly and softly than the first time.

"Careful, Recruit. You're going to set my heart monitor off. The nurses will come running."

Brooke smiled as she kissed her again. "I'll take my chances."

Chapter Fourteen

It had been two weeks since Homeland Security had arrived, and the Farm had been turned upside down with the investigation. They'd been interrogating Thompson for twenty hours a day and had yet to break him down. Homeland Security had agreed to do the questioning at the facility, deciding that the fewer times they had to transport the prisoner, the better. Brooke and the other members of her team had been given a passing score for their final mission. Seeing as they'd had to deal with an actual crisis, the grading board thought they handled it better than could have been expected. No one had been given a permanent assignment to date because the director had halted all orders until he was satisfied that the investigation had yielded all necessary results. If there were CIA people involved, he needed to know about it.

Brooke walked into the listening portion of the interrogation room. Patrick nodded in her direction as she entered.

"Anything new?"

He stretched and yawned. "No, nothing. Every time someone asks him a question, he starts singing a different Christmas carol. It's fucking annoying."

Brooke picked up the thin file and flipped through it. She had pored through these pages close to a hundred times and still wasn't able to find the missing link. They had determined that Thompson had a half brother who had been assigned to Tyler's unit, and he'd been killed during Tyler's last mission with the Marines. But none of that explained the number of men he had with him, nor the reason he was headed for the training mission facility.

"I heard the sergeant gets out today."

Brooke continued to flip through the pages, trying to hide her smile. "She does."

She could feel her face flushing hot, and despite her best efforts, she knew Patrick could see it too. Tyler had been recovering at an astounding rate the last few weeks, and the doctors had said yesterday she would be released into the care of a loved one this afternoon. Brooke would have loved nothing more than to be able to take care of Tyler herself, but that wasn't feasible. She resided in a barracks room at the Farm, which wasn't conducive to taking care of someone. Plus, it was an opportunity for Tyler to spend time with her aunt, who had rented a two-bedroom suite at a hotel near the Farm where she and Tyler would be staying for the next week or so. Brooke planned to spend as much time there as possible.

Jennifer came through the door with a stack of files, dropped them on the desk, and shook her head. "It would be so much faster if we were able to cross-check these with computers." It was a rhetorical statement. Everyone knew it was true, but the system had been breached, and it would still be three more days until they would be able to use it again, making their research move at a snail's pace.

"How is it working with the investigator from Homeland?"

Jennifer huffed. "Don't you mean God's gift to interrogation? I swear if they would let us take the lead, we would be able to move through this a lot faster."

"Is that so, Analyst Glass?"

Jennifer closed her eyes.

Their Homeland Security counterpart had just come through the door and had obviously overheard the conversation.

"I just think we may be going too easy on him, ma'am."

Special Agent Caden Styles sighed. "We weren't able to get any useful information out of his men. They were all kept in the dark intentionally. The computer scans we were able to run turned up absolutely nothing, and he has no prior convictions. There's nothing in his office or on any of his computers. If we don't walk the line with this, he could get off on a technicality."

Patrick crossed his arms. "Attempting to kill a gunnery sergeant and breaking into a CIA facility aren't enough?"

Styles leaned against the glass and rolled her eyes. "Obviously, we have more than enough to arrest him, and we can put him in jail for attempted murder, but what does that solve or prevent? We need to know *why*. Why is the most important question. You four should know that better than anyone, or was your entire year here a waste?" Her question didn't require an actual answer. She looked at Brooke, who had begun going through the files that Glass had brought in. "I want you to go in with me this time, Hart."

Brooke looked up, stunned. "Why?"

"He hasn't seen you since that night, and I'm hoping your presence will throw him off his game."

Brooke stood up. "Of course, whatever you need."

Styles nodded and they headed out the door and into the adjoining room.

The interrogation room was lit differently from the attached unit on the other side of the mirror. It had harsh, bright lighting and cement walls that were cold and looming. The air was stale and musty, like an old basement. Thompson was sitting with his eyes closed when they took their seats.

Brooke spoke first. "Hi, Michael."

Thompson's eyes opened, focusing on Brooke. "Well, well, if it isn't my pretty little bitch from the woods."

"I hoped you would remember me." Brooke planned on toying with him. She thought maybe the way to do it was through his libido.

Thompson pulled his arms up, stopping when the chains went taut. "Sorry I couldn't get more dressed up for you. I've been dreaming about you, the way your skin tasted of fear, the smell of your sweat." He closed his eyes and licked his lips. "I almost can't decide who I want more, you or Monroe."

Brooke made sure no change came over her face, though she wanted to pull his eyes out with her pen at the mention of Tyler. "And what did you decide?"

He leaned forward to speak, and his breath smelled of days with no brushing and limited water. "I want you both. Maybe at the same time." He leaned back in his chair, studying Brooke's face.

"Why Monroe? Why not just me?"

He squinted and one side of his mouth pushed up in an arrogant smirk. "Nicely played."

Brooke held eye contact. "I don't know what you mean."

He cocked his head to the side. "Don't you? You didn't make it this far without having a brain in that pretty head of yours."

Agent Styles stood up. "Let's go get some dinner, Hart."

❖

Tyler had finally made it back to the hotel, drenched in sweat and feeling like Jell-O. Walking to the corner store should have been a simple task, but it had completely wiped her out. *Shower and nap. Then I'll be fine.* She turned on the water and removed her clothes carefully. She stood and looked at herself in the mirror. The stitches closing the knife wound and marking the spot where her spleen had been repaired had started to dissolve, but both the physical and emotional scars would remain. She ran her fingers over the top of the red cut, admiring her healing abilities. Then she looked down at her leg. *Another bullet wound, another near miss.* She absently wondered if it was luck or a cruel joke that kept her alive time after time. Before Brooke, she assumed it was cruelty, but now, it was different. Maybe she was lucky after all.

Her aunt knocked on the door. "Do you need help, sweetie?"

Tyler felt the water. "No, I'm okay, thank you."

"Are you still seeing that psychiatrist, honey?"

Tyler sighed. "Yes, Aunt Claire, I still talk to her on the phone once a month."

"Maybe you should think about increasing the frequency? I mean after all this, that is."

"Yeah, maybe."

She knew her aunt would remain at the door listening for the next several minutes to ensure that there were no signs of distress, and the thought made her smile as she stepped into the hot spray. Her aunt was right. She was probably going to have to talk about this at length. The thought didn't scare her the way it had after Iraq. *Maybe I am making progress.* Tyler leaned forward, letting the water wash over her head and back. She placed her hands against the wall, partially to help take the weight off her leg and partially to steady her mind. Quiet times were always the most invasive. Small bits of clotted blood from her healing wounds swirled in the drain, and Tyler let her mind wander to the desert of Iraq. The pain she was feeling now, in her body and in the deepest parts of her psyche, always led back to that day in Iraq. *Lance Corporal Brown.* She didn't dare say his name out loud. His face flashed in her mind, but it didn't hold the same regret as the others, and she shuddered at the memory of him.

When Brooke arrived with pizza, Tyler was standing in front of a full-length mirror, attempting to place bandages on her body while balancing on one weak leg. Brooke hurried over.

"What are you doing? Let me help you."

Tyler sighed, exasperated with her futile attempts. "I didn't want to bother my aunt. I feel like all she's been doing is worrying about me."

Brooke eased Tyler back onto the bed. "Lie down and let me help you."

Tyler did as she was asked, aware that she was only in underwear and a bra, but Brooke's concentration was on the bandages rather than her body.

Brooke finished with her task, and Tyler watched her expression change from concentration to arousal. She watched Brooke's eyes move up and down her body. Tyler didn't feel judged or critiqued; the stare was a caress. Then Brooke's mind seemed to switch gears, and she grabbed the shirt that was laid out on the bed and handed it to Tyler.

"Put this on."

Tyler grabbed her arm. "Don't." Tyler watched Brooke take an obvious breath. "Lie down with me." Brooke looked like she wanted to protest, but Tyler already knew what she was thinking. "I'm not made of porcelain, honey." Brooke let out a deep breath and nodded. She kicked off her shoes and climbed into bed next to Tyler.

Brooke placed her head in the crook of Tyler's shoulder

with Tyler's arm around her body. "I've dreamt about this so many times."

Tyler kissed her forehead. "I hope you have imagined more than this."

Brooke gently pinched her leg and managed to speak in a half-joking tone. "Don't even start talking about that right now. Thinking about it will drive me insane."

Tyler ran her hand down Brooke's arm. "Having you this close is driving me insane."

She whispered, "Kiss me."

Brooke placed a hand on the side of Tyler's face and moved her mouth barely against hers. "I love you, Tyler."

Tyler pulled Brooke into a hot, fierce kiss, recognition of what they felt for each other clear in their touch. There were things she needed to say, things they needed to talk about. But now, in this moment, she wanted nothing more than the sensual feeling of Brooke's body against hers. The other stuff could wait.

Brooke's hand shook against Tyler's face as their tongues met and the intensity deepened. Brooke broke the kiss, with her forehead still against Tyler's. Breathlessly, she said, "We have to stop."

Tyler placed her hands on Brooke's face and kissed each cheek, then each eyelid. "I don't ever want to stop."

Brooke looked at her pleadingly. "Please, baby, I don't want to hurt you. You need time to heal."

Tyler kissed her neck and moved slowly up to the bottom of her ear. Brooke's breath hitched, and her body shuddered, and Tyler teasingly said, "I'll let you off the hook...for now."

As if on cue, there was a knock at the door. "Girls, I really need you two to eat."

Tyler smiled. "It's like being a teenager all over again."

Brooke gave her a faux-angry grimace. "Just how many girls have you been caught with in your room, Gunnery Sergeant?"

Tyler grinned and pushed her body up, carefully pulling on sweats and a tank top. "Let's get some pizza before I get myself into trouble."

"Uh-huh." Brooke pinched her again.

Dinner was oddly domestic, with Claire telling stories of a young Tyler. The deep love she had for her was frosted all over every word she spoke. Tyler rolled her eyes and pretended to be bothered by her doting, all the while a smile never leaving her face.

"How do your parents feel about what you do, Brooke?"

Brooke sat back and twisted the wine glass in her hand. "They aren't fully aware of what I do."

Tyler interjected when Claire looked ready to protest. "Remember that you only know because of the situation we're in."

Brooke shook her head. "It's not that. I'm trained to be an analyst. I'm not a clandestine agent. I could fill them in on *what* I do, just not the details. I'm just not sure they're all that interested."

Claire said, "Oh, honey, I'm sure they are very proud of you."

Brooke took a sip of wine and shrugged. "My mother believes that an MIT degree is wasted on a government job and that I should be in Corporate America, looking for a husband."

Claire was clearly taken aback. "Your parents don't know you're gay?"

Brooke finished off the last of her wine and set the empty glass on the table. "Not because I haven't told them. They just refuse to hear me."

Claire covered Brooke's hand with her own. "It's their

loss, honey, and if I ever have the chance to meet them, I'll let them know as much."

Tyler watched Brooke carefully to gauge her reaction. There was no hate or anger, just acceptance. She took Brooke's hand and rubbed the back of it with her thumb. She was about to speak when Brooke's phone rang.

She glanced down at the caller ID, looked back at Tyler, and said, "I'm sorry. I have to take this." Tyler nodded and Brooke walked into the bedroom. Tyler kissed her aunt's cheek. "I'm going to go back to bed."

"Good night, sweetheart. See you in the morning."

Brooke was still on the phone when Tyler entered the room. She leaned against the door and watched Brooke's concentration on the conversation she was having. One of the reasons Tyler had fallen in love with Brooke was being captured in that moment. Brooke stayed focused on whoever was speaking on the other end as she methodically took off her clothes and folded them perfectly into a little pile before placing them on top of her bag. Tyler loved the way she gave things such complete attention. She pulled the toothbrush from one of the side pockets and sat on the bed, tapping the end to her cheek. After several moments, she said, "All I can promise is that I'll ask."

Fear and anger flashed in Brooke's eyes, and Tyler was pleased she was becoming so aware of Brooke's emotions.

"Agent Styles, I said I would ask." She hung up the phone and walked to the bathroom.

Tyler hobbled behind and leaned in the door frame of the bathroom. "Something the matter?"

Brooke looked at Tyler in the mirror as she brushed. "Agent Styles, with Homeland Security, has a request."

Tyler crossed her arms, trying not to laugh at Brooke's overly articulate identification of the person on the other end of the phone, evidence that she was beyond annoyed. "And I am assuming that you don't like the request."

Brooke seemed to brush harder on her teeth than necessary. "Thompson says he'll talk, but only to you."

Tyler contemplated the request silently.

Brooke spit out the toothpaste. "Baby, if you aren't ready to face him, we can just tell her no."

Tyler put her arms around Brooke, enjoying the sensation of her body in nothing more than a bra. "Is that what you would recommend?"

Without hesitation, she said, "Yes."

Tyler smiled at Brooke's inherent need to protect her. "What if I wasn't your girlfriend, what would you recommend then?"

Brooke wrapped her arms around Tyler's neck. "That's not fair."

"I'm not afraid to face him, Brooke. I'm far more afraid of what might happen if we don't know what he's up to."

Brooke rested her forehead on Tyler's shoulder. "I just don't like the idea of you anywhere near him after what happened."

Tyler kissed her head. "Brooke, honey, I'm a Marine. There will always be another Thompson to face, another enemy to confront. It's my job." And with those words, Tyler realized it was true. Her fears about no longer being a Marine were unfounded. She would always be a Marine, and she was proud to be one. No matter what that position entailed in the future, it was in her soul. The part of her agonizing over her identity for so long suddenly lightened, and she felt herself stand a little straighter.

Brooke turned back around and started to wash her face. "I didn't say you can't. I just said I don't like it."

"*I can't?*"

Brooke dried her hands on the towel. "You know what I mean, Tyler."

Tyler turned to walk out of the bathroom, and Brooke grabbed her arm. "I just mean that I almost lost you to him, and it's only been a few weeks. It just scares me."

"It's my job, Brooke."

Brooke nodded. "I know, and I wouldn't ask you to ever give it up. It will just take some getting used to." She moved back into Tyler's embrace. "Can we worry about my inability to let you out of my sight later?"

Tyler chuckled. "You aren't having a bubble made for me this very moment, are you?"

Brooke's face lit up. "What a great idea!" She led Tyler back to the bed and then turned around to face her. She gently put her hands under Tyler's tank top. "Let me help you."

Tyler's head was spinning. This was really happening. She nodded and slowly moved her arms up so that Brooke could remove her top. As soon as the clothing was over her head, Brooke's mouth was on her neck. Her soft lips sent shivers down her body,

"I know we shouldn't, but I can't stop myself. I have to touch you," she said between agonizing kisses up and down the column of Tyler's neck.

Tyler tried to gulp down her desire as she placed her hands on Brooke's back and slowly started stroking her up and down.

"Sit down."

Tyler did as she was instructed, and Brooke knelt, pulling the sweats down Tyler's legs, slowly, one leg at a time. Once she got them off, she crawled up along the other side of Tyler stroking the uninjured part of her stomach with a soft, intimate touch. Tyler watched as the fingertips moved up and down her abdomen, her muscles flinching the farther down Brooke's movements ventured.

"God, you're beautiful."

Tyler couldn't answer. She could only see Brooke's head move down to kiss her stomach, following the painfully arousing trail her fingertips had just left. Tyler laid her head back down on the pillow, feeling her body's reactions to Brooke caresses. Tyler placed her absolute concentration on not coming when Brooke's mouth reached her nipple and tugged gently with her teeth.

Tyler's involuntary reaction to Brooke only seemed to drive her further. Her hand slid down Tyler's hard torso, purposefully and slowly, discovering each contour. When her fingers slid underneath her panties and finally found the soft, slick wetness between Tyler's legs, a loud moan escaped Brooke's mouth, breathing hot, moist air onto Tyler's breast.

Tyler shivered and whispered Brooke's name.

Brooke slid two fingers into Tyler and slowly rubbed her clit with her thumb in a soft circle. Tyler's breathing increased, and her body began to engulf itself with a soft sheen of sweat. Brooke kissed her, then pushed between her legs harder and deeper than she had at first. Tyler cried out, covering Brooke's hand with warm wetness.

Tyler murmured, "I love you," into the darkness over and over again.

Brooke was still kissing her as Tyler's breathing eased. Her hips were involuntarily rocking as Tyler stroked her back. "Come here." She pushed Brooke's body up with one arm, guiding her into place with her legs on either side of her head.

Brooke gripped the headboard as Tyler kissed the inside of each leg. "Baby, I need to come." Brooke gasped as Tyler continued to take her time, enjoying the rich aroma that surrounded her.

When she finally reached the center of the heat, Tyler made one long movement with her tongue, up to the base of the soft, wet curls. Brooke gripped the headboard, and Tyler pulled down on her, placing Brooke's clit directly on her mouth. She began to suck gently, flicking the small fold back and forth with her tongue rhythmically. She slid her fingers into Brooke slowly as she listened to her whisper a variety of things that no one was meant to understand. Brooke's strong, perfect legs were shaking as Tyler softly bit down on her clit, and Brooke's whole body began to quiver as her orgasm overcame her and Tyler felt her wetness gush in response.

Brooke eased off Tyler and laid her head back down on her shoulder. Her body was still trembling. She absently traced circles on Tyler's chest. "I have never come like that, never wanted anyone so much or felt so connected."

Tyler kissed her forehead. "It's just the beginning. If you want me, of course."

Brooke tried not to laugh. "Tyler, I've been chasing you for almost two months. Do you honestly think I suddenly changed my mind, in this moment?"

Tyler was quiet, and Brooke wished she could read her mind. "Could you please tell me what's going on inside that head of yours?"

During the pause in conversation, Brooke was petrified. The possibilities of what could come out of Tyler's mouth were endless. Brooke braced herself for the words she thought would follow. Excuses about why they couldn't be together, reasons of why they could never be.

"I have nightmares, Brooke. Not just any nightmares. I relive things. I see things in my dreams like they're happening all over again."

Brooke restrained herself from squeezing her tighter for reassurance. She wanted Tyler to continue, and she was scared that if she changed any movement, Tyler would stop. So she remained quiet and totally still.

"I see their faces. I feel the heat from the bomb, the vehicle fire. It's like I'm right back there all over again. When I wake up, I'm not sure where I am. It even happens sometimes during the day. Like a fog I can't see through."

"Does it help to talk about it?"

Tyler shrugged. "I was seeing a shrink twice a week for a while. Now I talk to her once a month on the phone. I would like to say that it doesn't help, but it does. It has, even though I hate doing it."

Brooke kept calm, in direct conflict to everything she was feeling. Tyler was hurting, and that thought alone hurt her in a place she had never felt for another person. It thrummed in her chest. "It doesn't make you broken. It means you're healing."

Tyler looked down at her, and there seemed to be a genuine question in her eyes. "Do you think that's possible? To really ever heal from something like that? What if I don't know what I'm doing and I hurt you? I couldn't live with myself…"

Brooke took a moment to gather her response. She needed Tyler to believe her words, wanted her to know that she truly believed what she was going to tell her, and she needed to say just the right thing. "Yes, Tyler, I do. I think that bad, terrible things happen, things that can never be forgotten. Things that live inside us, shaping who we are and the decisions that we make. But can you heal from it? Yes. It will always be a part of you, but it doesn't have to be who you are." She sighed and shrugged. "I don't know that you won't hurt me. I don't believe you will. But the thought of not moving forward together because of an 'if' doesn't work for me."

Tyler smiled at her, and Brooke thought it was the most fantastic smile she had ever seen. Brooke kissed her slowly, wanting Tyler to feel every ounce of desire and love she felt for her. She pulled back with a groan. "I can't keep kissing you. I'm not going to be able to stop, and you desperately need your rest." Tyler kissed her again, exploring her mouth sensually, and Brooke groaned into Tyler's mouth. "Seriously, baby, we need to stop. I shouldn't have even let it get this far tonight."

"That's not what your body is saying."

Brooke bit her lower lip. She straddled Tyler's leg, coating her with her warm wetness that Tyler had once again inspired so quickly.

Tyler groaned at the contact, feeling her clit harden and swell as she watched Brooke rock slowly back and forth on her leg.

"I want to taste you."

Tyler's breathing rapidly increased as she watched Brooke move down her body again, her lips leaving a trail of goose bumps in their wake.

Tyler clung to the sheets as she watched Brooke's tongue trace its way over her hip bone, across the hollow of her stomach, and down to the inside of her leg. Brooke put her mouth to Tyler's warm, throbbing, slick folds. Tyler's voice shook as she urged her on.

Tyler's body was begging for release as it shivered on the bed, and Brooke placed her hands around Tyler's hips to hold her in place. As Brooke ran her tongue around the inside of her, Tyler couldn't stop the low rumbles of need, which seemed to push Brooke's own need further as her breath began to change and her body started to tremble. Brooke slid her own hand down between her legs as she sucked harder on Tyler's clit. Tyler's body became rigid as she called out Brooke's name and came in her mouth.

Brooke rested her head against the inside of Tyler's leg,

her body coated with sex and sweat. Tyler's body trembled with satisfaction, and she looked down at Brooke, who was smiling back with what could only be described as accomplishment.

Tyler said, still trying to catch her breath, "Please come lie with me."

Brooke moved up beside her, again resting her head on Tyler's shoulder. Tyler realized right before she fell asleep that this was the first time since she could remember that her mind was truly at peace.

CHAPTER FIFTEEN

Brooke woke up ten minutes before her alarm was set to go off. She stared at the bedside clock, thinking about the feel of Tyler's body next to her own. She wanted to stay here all day, to make love a dozen more times, but that wasn't possible right now. She needed to get to work so they could make progress and get this behind them. She rolled over and reluctantly got out of bed, making her way to the bathroom after a long glance at Tyler's sleeping form beneath the sheets.

Brooke turned on the water and stared in the mirror. Images of the night before flooded her mind. She smiled as she retraced the places that Tyler had kissed and touched. Her skin smelled like a mixture of both of their bodies, and her nipples hardened with the memory. She let out a deep sigh and got into the shower. The water felt good on her painfully sensitive skin as the physical remnants from the night before disappeared down the drain, leaving only the emotional gratification behind.

She walked into the bedroom and began to dress for the day, unaware that Tyler was watching until she spoke.

"You're amazing."

Brooke smiled at her as she pulled her pants on.

"You're pretty incredible yourself." Brooke started tying her boots.

"You sure you don't want to get back in bed with me?" Tyler asked.

"I would love to, but if I go anywhere near that bed, I won't be making it in to work today."

Tyler sat up slowly, still favoring the side where her sutures were healing. The sheet fell off her body, leaving her naked and beautiful.

Brooke couldn't help but stare. "Don't try to distract me, Sergeant."

Tyler stood and limped over to where Brooke was sitting. "I wouldn't dream of it, Analyst Hart."

Love and emotion were etched in Tyler's crystal blue eyes, and Brooke fell in love all over again. "God, I love you."

Tyler smiled and kissed Brooke, a kiss soaked in future promises and adventures unseen. "I love you too."

Tyler walked slowly to the bathroom. "I'll be coming down a little later today."

Brooke froze. She still didn't like the idea of Tyler being anywhere near Thompson, regardless of the need.

Tyler stopped and looked back at her when she didn't respond. "Brooke, it's something I have to do, and we need answers."

Brooke nodded. She didn't have to like it. Tyler headed into the shower and Brooke went out the door. It was still far too early for Claire to be up, so Brooke left a quick note on the counter thanking her for her hospitality and left for the day. Today wouldn't be like the last several hundred she had spent at Camp Peary. It wouldn't even be like the last fifteen. Tyler would be there today, and not just any version of Tyler. A healing, unrecovered Tyler. Her Tyler. She let Tyler's reassurance play though her head. They needed answers, and she could get them. Brooke needed to put her personal feelings aside. Tyler was right. This was her job and she was good at it. She could have her career and her love. She just had to remain focused.

❖

Brooke walked into the monitoring room, where Patrick, Jennifer, and Chris had already started their day. Everyone was quiet when she sat down and looked around the room. "What?" She set down the bag of donuts that she had brought for everyone.

Jennifer opened the bag and pulled out one of the sugar-coated treats. "You didn't come back to the room last night."

Brooke felt her face immediately blush. "We don't have a curfew anymore. We aren't recruits."

Jennifer shrugged. "I know. Just making an observation."

Brooke walked over to the board that was covered in maps, pictures of possible targets, pictures of people, and Post-its, and stared, but she could feel Jennifer's eyes on her.

"There's something different about you."

Brooke crossed her arms. "Oh my God, would you three please knock it off and focus."

Jennifer put up her hands in surrender. "Okay, okay. I just have one question for you."

Brooke shook her head. "What?"

"Is she as good in bed as she looks like she would be?"

Laughter engulfed the room as Brooke tried to hide her embarrassment.

The door swung open and Special Agent Styles strode in. "What's so funny?"

All four responded in unison, "Nothing."

Patrick broke the silence. "Anything new?"

Jennifer shook her head. "I know we're missing something. I just can't figure out what."

Patrick nodded his agreement. "I know what you mean. I feel like it is staring us in the face, but I can't put my finger on it."

Jennifer continued to sip her coffee as she stared at the wall. "Maybe we're asking the wrong questions."

Agent Styles grabbed a donut out of the bag and stood next to Brooke, staring at the board. "Did you talk to her?"

"Yes, she's coming in today to speak to him. But I don't think—"

Styles turned to the others. "Sergeant Monroe will be coming in today to speak with the prisoner. Let's be on our A game. We don't want to miss anything if she gets him talking."

❖

Hate wasn't a strong enough word for what Tyler felt about being stuck in a wheelchair, but her vocabulary lacked a better word. The director met her halfway down the hall and Tyler said, "I don't like being pushed around in this thing." The recruit pushing her laughed softly.

The director chuckled. "You aren't healed enough for crutches yet, and I can't have you tripping around here just to prove what a badass you are."

Tyler shot him an unappreciative glare. Nicole took over for the recruit as they made the final turn into the underground tunnel that would lead to where Thompson was being held. Tyler had never been in this part of the facility, but she wasn't surprised it existed.

"We miss you," Nicole said.

Tyler reached back and touched Nicole's hand. "I miss you too."

The director pushed the door open, and Nicole wheeled Tyler through the entrance. The faces of her recruits brought an unexpected sense of relief. She'd known they were all okay, but actually seeing them made her feel much better.

Jennifer Glass was the first to reach her. "I'm so glad you're okay." She leaned down and kissed her on the cheek, and let her mouth linger for longer than necessary. When she turned around smiling, Brooke quickly shot her a warning look.

Agent Styles cut off the reunion quickly. "I appreciate you coming in. We need to go over what exactly you're going to say."

Tyler looked at the woman, who seemed to be trying to overcompensate for something. "You must be Agent Styles. I don't know what I'm going to say. I'll go in there and see where the conversation leads."

Styles clearly wasn't on board with that particular strategy and looked about to protest.

"I'll wear an earpiece, but that's the best I can do."

Styles glanced at the director, who raised his eyebrows and shrugged.

"Fine." Styles stalked off to find the equipment she needed.

Brooke went to Tyler's side to help her out of the cumbersome wheelchair.

"I really don't like this," Brooke whispered to Tyler, not wanting anyone else to sense her unease.

"It'll be fine." Tyler smiled, trying to reassure her. "But I am walking in. I won't let him see me in a wheelchair."

Agent Styles handed the earpiece to Tyler. "I assume you don't need help putting this in."

Tyler cocked her head. "No, I think I can handle it." She placed the device in her ear, and Patrick spoke into the microphone, testing to make sure it was working. She gave a thumbs-up. She winked at Brooke and limped out.

Before she opened the next door to the interrogation room, she took a deep breath, bracing herself for what was next. She entered and made eye contact with Thompson. A wicked smile crossed his face as she went to sit down.

"Gunnery Sergeant Monroe. How have you been?"

"I've been fine, thank you for asking. How is your leg?"

He shrugged and looked down. "Not my worst injury."

"I'm sorry to hear that." Her face remained unchanged as she stared into his eyes. "I'm told you wanted to speak with me."

"How is Ms. Hart?"

He was baiting her, but there was no way she'd let him get to her. "I believe she's fine. I haven't had the opportunity to spend much time with her."

He looked at her sideways. "You don't honestly expect me to believe that, do you?"

"I don't really care what you believe."

He leaned forward. "Why did you change places with her?"

"I would have traded places with any one of the recruits."

"Would you?" His voice was dripping in sarcasm.

"Yes."

"I want to talk about my brother."

"I want to talk about why you broke into Camp Peary. So, since we both want something, what do you say we trade information?"

He thought about it for a moment. "You let him die."

Tyler shook her head. "Is that what you think?"

"It's what I know."

"What were you after when you came here?" She could play this game as well.

"You ruined his reputation, destroyed his good name, and then you let him die in the desert, alone."

"He ruined his own reputation." She kept her voice even and steady in contrast to his growing anger, which seemed to be making him even crazier. "Were you trying to plant a bomb?"

He scoffed. "A bomb? Ha! No, that's a futile act, on a place that holds no real importance." He paused. "Why did you let him die?"

Tyler leaned forward and crossed her hands on the table. "Your brother is the reason that everyone died. I should have seen it coming and had him removed from the unit, but I didn't, and that's on me."

"My brother is a fucking hero! You're the reason that everyone died, not him!" He was pounding his fists on the table, but Tyler remained unmoved.

"Your brother was a rapist piece of shit that sold out his own unit. He hadn't planned to be with us that day. I made him come because I didn't trust him to be back at camp without my supervision. He paid an Iraqi insurgent to plant that bomb on that specific road to have us all killed so there would be no one to testify at his court-martial hearing. It was his bad luck he ended up being in the vehicle with us."

Fury was radiating off his body. "You're a damn liar!" Thompson raged, spittle flying onto the table between them. "Their blood is on your hands. You're fucking covered in it!"

Tyler shook her head. "I don't know why I'm surprised. I should have figured you wouldn't be any different. Blood follows blood. You had no real purpose coming here. You were looking for me. Anything beyond that isn't possible for a piece of crap like you."

"You have no idea what you're talking about."

"Don't I? Remember, I worked with your brother. It's not

possible for anyone in your family to be smart enough to break in here without being caught. You wanted to be caught…by me."

"What I have planned…it will change this country, this world, forever."

Tyler rolled her eyes. "Please. Your brother drugged, raped, and beat female soldiers, and got caught doing it. You actually expect me to believe that in the other part of the family there's a criminal mastermind at work?"

He started to thrash in his chair. "You have no fucking idea what I am capable of! Undo these cuffs and I'll show you what I can fucking do."

A voice came through Tyler's earpiece. "Take a break for a few minutes. Let him work himself up, and then we'll push him for more details."

Tyler yawned. "I'm bored. I'm going to go get a cup of coffee. When I get back, we can keep talking about how you were single-handedly going to take down the entire United States." She laughed as she walked out the door. When it shut behind her, she leaned over, gripping her knees and fighting the need to vomit. Images of her unit, her team from that day, flooded her senses once again. She could hear the short screams, smell the burnt flesh, and see the flames licking at the vehicle. She ran a hand over her face and took three deep breaths. Once the nausea was at bay and she could see beyond the desert images, she pushed open the door to the next room.

Brooke took one look at Tyler and filled a small paper cup with water and set it in front of her. Tyler drank, not because she was thirsty, but because she needed something to stay occupied.

Agent Styles walked up to Tyler. "We need an end game. And we need to know who's behind it."

They sat without speaking for some time. Tyler tried to

push the memories to the back of her mind. She'd deal with them later. Right now, she needed to stay focused. Brooke's foot touched hers under the table, and she gave her a small, grateful smile. Patrick handed her a cup of coffee and she got to her feet. "Let's do it."

She opened the door to the next room and took her seat again. She set her coffee on the table after taking an appreciate sniff of it. "There, that's better. Now maybe I can keep myself awake through all your babbling. You were saying?"

"I was saying that you're a dumb dyke bitch." He spat on the ground to emphasize his apparent hatred.

Tyler gave him a patronizing smile. "Very creative. Now, it was stupid for you to come in the way you did when I would normally have been in my quarters that time of night. Did you get the map all turned around?" She sipped her coffee, keeping her expression neutral. She saw it in his eyes. He knew exactly what she was doing. The question now was whether his arrogance would force him to tell the truth, or if he'd play dumb to protect his ultimate mission. Tyler was positive it would be the first.

"If I wanted you dead, you would be."

"Well, we both know that's not true, since I'm sitting here having this conversation with you." She paused briefly. "You had me unarmed and at gunpoint, and yet here I sit. Does your inability to perform properly happen in other aspects of your life too?"

He pounded his fists on the table as the veins in his neck started protruding. Sweat beaded on his forehead and upper lip. "Why don't you unchain me and I'll show you just how well I perform!"

Tyler got out of her seat and walked around the table. She sat down close enough for him to grab her if he decided to. She was pushing him, showing she had no fear.

"The next step is to pull your mother into one of these rooms to see what she knows. Before you protest as to whether or not we're allowed to take such action, I suggest you think back to all of the options the Patriot Act allows us." She sipped her coffee again. "How do you think she would take to these conditions? It would probably be really hard on her, knowing that one son is a rapist and the other, well, the other just simply doesn't love her enough to protect her."

"You keep my mother out of this." The fear in his face was genuine. Panic was starting to set in. He looked around the room, as if trying to find an escape hatch.

That's the key. The mother. Tyler thought back to the file and all the details about his family. She'd use what she had to in order to get what they needed. He put both palms over his eyes, and Tyler couldn't tell if he was crying or inflicting pain on himself. She realized it didn't really matter to her which it was. "Here's what we are going to do. The people behind that glass wall are going to send someone to your mother's house. We are going to drag her out in handcuffs and toss her in the back of a car. Then they are going to bring her here and toss her in a room with no windows, no doors, no way out." His body was shaking now, and Tyler knew she was almost there. "After a period of time"—she forced a chuckle and shook her head—"which, let's be honest, no one knows how long that will be, I will go into that room and I will show your mother the pictures of every single woman your brother brutalized. Every injury, every bruise, every bleeding wound, everything." He was quiet now, motionless. "When she says she's had enough and asks why we're doing this to her, I'm going to show her a picture of you. I'm going to tell her that you let us, that you wanted us to, that we told you our plans and you would rather sacrifice her than yourself."

His voice was quiet, defeated. "You can't do that. You won't do that."

"Are you sure you want to take that chance?"

He sat silently for a long while, and Tyler let him be. She sat back down, her leg and side throbbing. She'd let him consider because she knew he wouldn't take the risk.

"I'll tell you what you want to know, but I have a few conditions." His palms continued to cover his eyes.

"You aren't really in a position to be making deals."

"All I want is for the death penalty to be taken off the table and for you to leave my mother alone. She's not to be questioned. Get me those things in writing and I'll tell you what you want, including who I was working with inside the CIA."

Tyler was losing her battle in trying to fight off her growing anger. "Now you're lying."

He pulled his palms away and looked directly into her eyes. "Am I? Are you sure you want to take that chance?" There was a knock on the window and he spoke again. "Get it in writing and I'll tell you everything." Then he sat back in his chair and began to hum "Jingle Bells."

CHAPTER SIXTEEN

This is bullshit! He's a traitor! Are we really not going to seek the death penalty?" Brooke said.

Agent Styles had her phone pressed to her ear and barely glanced at Brooke. "It's not your call, Hart. Sometimes sacrifices have to be made for the greater good. Look at the bigger picture."

"We're the CIA! As soon as we have access to our computer systems, we'll be able to determine who he has been working with. We don't need him to tell us," Brooke said, her voice rising.

Agent Styles was still on hold, waiting to be put through to her superior. "You're a naïve little girl." She turned away to indicate the conversation was over.

Brooke took a step toward her, thinking of her combat training with Tyler. One swift kick…

Nicole put a hand on Brooke's shoulder and held her in place. She gave her a warning look before saying to Styles, "What if you give us forty-eight hours? If we can't determine the unknown variables in forty-eight hours, Homeland Security can do whatever needs to be done."

Styles tapped her pencil on the desk and hung up the phone. She pointed at Nicole. "Forty-eight hours, that's it."

Brooke stomped from the room to head to the analyst center. Nicole caught up and held her back with a hand on her shoulder.

"This is bullshit! If this were Langley, our system would have been back up in two hours and we would never be in this situation." Brooke ran her hands through her hair in frustration, not knowing what else to do with them. *Punching Styles would make me feel better.* "If the director had made some phone calls, we could have gotten the support we needed, been patched through to their system." She brushed off Nicole's hand and paced. She couldn't get out her frustration.

Nicole crossed her arms. "Are you done?"

Brooke leaned against the wall and shoved her hands in her pockets. "Go ahead."

"Requesting assistance from CIA headquarters in Langley would have brought this investigation out of our walls and opened up a whole new set of problems."

Brooke looked away but was still listening. She didn't want to hear reason right now. She wanted to punch Styles and then force the investigation forward.

"Plus, if there is a breach within the CIA, you have no idea where or how far up that goes, and if it left this facility, it would give someone the opportunity to cover the whole thing up. The director took a huge chance by allowing us to work on this situation and demanded that we only have one Homeland Security agent assigned, purposely downplaying the whole incident until we know what's going on. If we aren't able to pull this off, he'll lose his job."

Brooke leaned against the wall and looked up, closing her eyes. "It was just...it was personal. He attacked Tyler, one of our own. He can't get away with that."

Nicole wrapped an arm around Brooke's shoulders. "Tyler is fine, and if you really want to help protect her, you need to pull it together and do your job so we can figure out exactly who we're dealing with." Nicole gave her a quick hug and headed back to the interrogation unit. "He's going to prison, Brooke. He's just not going to die. Wise up."

Brooke took a deep breath and headed for the analyst center. Nicole was right. It was time to put her personal feelings aside, as much as possible, and get to work.

❖

Patrick said, for the umpteenth time, "We need to work in shifts."

Brooke shook her head. "It's only forty-eight hours. We need to get through this."

Patrick pulled Brooke's chair backward, away from her keyboard. "We're going to start duplicating work."

Brooke pushed herself back to her keyboard. "Then take a break, Patrick."

Jennifer walked into the room balancing three cups of coffee in her hands. She handed one to Patrick and one to Brooke. "Find anything?"

Patrick shook his head. "I think we need to work in shifts."

"And I said go ahead and take a break. I'm not going anywhere," Brooke said. "There, right there. What's that?"

Jennifer pointed to the large screen. "Freeze that and zoom in." Brooke did as she was asked. The software had been scanning the computer devices that they had confiscated from Thompson's men. All the hard drives had been wiped, but Brooke had been working on retrieving the files while Patrick had been trying to locate and evaluate encryption bytes, and there had been trace fragments left on several of the computers. "That's it. We need to drill this down."

Jennifer pulled up her chair. "Hart, this is my area of

expertise. Take a break. This is going to take hours." Jennifer started pounding on the keyboard, engulfed in the lead she was chasing.

❖

Brooke went outside for fresh air and to clear her head. She had mindlessly started wandering, the movement refreshing after sitting for almost ten hours. She saw Tyler sitting on a bench alone and gladly headed that direction. "I thought you would have already headed back."

Tyler shook her head. "No, I'd just sit there and think about what's going on here."

Brooke kissed her on the cheek. "You need to rest."

Tyler took her hand and smiled down at their entwined fingers. "I'll rest when this is over."

"You can go lie down in your quarters."

Tyler shook her head.

"Your nightmares are worse, aren't they?"

Tyler continued to rub Brooke's hand absently. "I'm a rational, logical person. I know that what happened wasn't my fault, but they were my responsibility and that's something that won't change, no matter how much we talk about it. I failed them, and I very nearly failed all of you when I left you alone at the training mission. It's like the two situations keep combining and I can't make out which is which. And in all of them...I can't save you."

Brooke kissed Tyler's cheek. "It's not about changing what happened, honey. It's about accepting that it did happen, and that there's nothing you can do to change it now. And it's about knowing that everything is okay with the team and with us. I'm here, next to you. Safe because you saved my life."

Tyler's shoulders hunched and she whispered, "Moving on feels like forgetting."

Brooke placed her hand on the side of her face and kissed her. "You owe it to them to move on, to be happy. You have to stop punishing yourself for a bomb you didn't plant and for a situation you couldn't control. No one could have stopped what happened."

Tears started streaming down Tyler's cheeks, and she covered her face with her hands.

"Oh, honey." Brooke wrapped her in an embrace and slowly rocked her back and forth. Her heart broke for Tyler, what she was feeling, what she had to endure, but mostly for the tremendous heart she possessed, which was so badly bruised. "What do you say we take a break for a little while?"

"I would like that." Tyler wiped her tears on her sleeve and followed Brooke back to her old quarters.

Once they were ensconced behind closed doors, Brooke said, "Take off your clothes and lie down with me."

Tyler did as she was asked and crawled into bed.

Brooke took what was quickly becoming her normal spot with her head on Tyler's shoulder. "How are you feeling?"

Tyler kissed Brooke's forehead. "Much, much better now that I'm here with you."

"Oh yeah?" Brooke said softly. "Is there anything that I can do to make you feel even better?" She started aimlessly stroking Tyler's stomach.

"How much time do we have?"

Brooke chuckled. "Enough."

Tyler leaned down and kissed Brooke deeply. "I'm not sure there is such thing when it comes to you."

Brooke inhaled, loving the way Tyler's mouth felt on hers, the way her tongue entered her, claiming her. Tyler's hand moved up Brooke's side, grazing the outside of her breast. Brooke reacted by pushing herself closer. "Tell me if I hurt you." Brooke straddled Tyler's waist. She slowly moved her hips downward, coming briefly in contact with Tyler's center. Brooke was instantly wet and throbbing. She placed her hands on either side of Tyler's head and started kissing her neck, slowly grinding her hips into Tyler's.

She opened her legs wider until their clits touched and rubbed each other in unison. A shudder traveled through her body, her arms tensing, struggling to keep her weight up. "Oh my God, that feels so good." Brooke pushed harder into Tyler, their slick folds sliding into one another, over and over again.

Tyler lifted up, putting her mouth on Brooke's nipple, and Brooke pushed her chest further into Tyler, as she sucked and pulled. Her voice became louder, her panting more urgent with each movement. Just as Brooke thought she was close, so close, Tyler slid her hand between her legs, finding the hard clit easily. She slid it between her fingers and squeezed. Brooke came hard and fast, pumping her hips into Tyler, coating her.

Wave after wave washed over them both until Brooke could no longer hold herself up, and she fell to Tyler's side, panting. She wiped the hair out of her eyes. "Do you think it will ever take us longer than a few minutes?"

Tyler let out an appreciative sound. "Maybe one day, but not any time soon."

Brooke kissed Tyler's bare breast. "I'm okay with that."

"Mmm...me too."

Brooke's phone rang. She got up and searched her pockets for the ringing device. She looked at the caller ID and answered. "Nicole...yeah, on my way." She closed the phone and started dressing quickly.

Tyler pushed herself up and carefully started pulling on her clothes. "What's up?"

"I have to get back down there. They found something. Are you okay?"

Tyler wiggled her eyebrows. "Better than okay. I'll meet you down there. Get going."

Brooke tied her shoes, straightened her shirt, and checked her hair in the mirror. "Do I look like I just had sex?"

Tyler laughed. "Either that or like you worked out."

Brooke kissed her on the cheek. "Perfect. Love you." She was out the door.

❖

Brooke walked into the room adjacent to the analyst center. She was stacking several folders in her arms to take over to Nicole and Jennifer. She was only half listening to the monitoring system humming with their voices. She glanced up at the screen when she heard a beep that indicated someone was using their key fob to enter the analyst room.

Chris Carlson walked in, looked at the large screen, and pulled out his sidearm. He pointed it at Jennifer and Nicole. "Both of you, against the wall. Now."

Brooke dropped the folders but couldn't take her eyes off the screen. She felt paralyzed. She forced her hand to move, and it bumped the phone receiver on the desk. She picked it up, barely allowing herself to glance down, and punched in four numbers. "Sir, you need to get down to the office next to the analyst room. Now."

Brooke was shocked to see the door open yet again, and Agent Styles entered the room, having used her back to open the door, holding a box of chicken chow mein. "This better be good." She turned around and looked directly at Jennifer and Nicole, who stood with their backs against the wall. She followed their line of vision, and judging by the tone in her voice, was as shocked as everyone else. "Analyst Carlson? What the hell are you doing?"

"You too." He used his weapon to gesture toward the wall. "Come on." He walked over, keeping his gun trained on his three hostages. "Give me your gun."

Styles went to reach for it. "Wait, no, stop." She put her hands back up in the air. "I'll grab it." As he was approaching, it must have occurred to him that he would have to get within arm's distance to take her weapon. He was clearly getting frustrated with himself. "Just take it off and slide it over here. But don't do anything stupid."

Brooke knew Styles wasn't going to do anything but exactly what he said. He had clearly forgotten that there was no scenario in which this ended well for him. Styles didn't need to do anything but wait.

"You do realize that you have taken three hostages." She slid her gun across the floor. "In a room that is not only frequented by several people an hour but has cameras everywhere."

Panic seemed to be starting to set in, and he repeatedly hit his head with his hand. "Shit, shit, shit," he muttered as he paced the room.

Nicole shook her head. "Why, Chris? Why did you do this?"

He flipped around quickly, his face starting to shine with sweat. "He wasn't supposed to get caught, and I was supposed to make a million bucks."

Jennifer took a step forward. "You were willing to kill the sergeant for a million dollars? What the hell is wrong with you?"

He turned the gun in her direction, forcing her back against the wall. "No! I didn't know anything about the sergeant. All I had to do was stick a thumb drive into our system for a few hours. I didn't know anything about anything else. You have to believe me."

Nicole held her hands up. "I believe you, Chris, but you aren't making things any easier on yourself by doing this."

He was rubbing his head with his palm, "I can't go to jail. I can't."

"It's a little late for that." Nicole and Jennifer shot Styles a nasty look. "What?" She shrugged. "I mean seriously, is that thing even loaded with real bullets?" Styles took a step forward, and Carlson shot the gun into the ceiling. White debris started falling to the ground. "I guess so." She stepped back against the wall.

"Did you really think that you were going to get away with this?"

Carlson shook his head. "It was never supposed to get this far."

Styles chuckled. "Did you really think that someone was willing to pay a million dollars for useless information? You had to assume they were buying something valuable."

He screamed back. "I didn't know what they were buying!"

Jennifer shook her head. "Oh, Chris. What have you done?"

"Shut up! All of you, shut up!" He pounded his free hand against his head again.

❖

Director Broadus, Patrick, and Kyle had made it into the room and were standing with Brooke, riveted to the monitors. The director took a step back and picked up his phone, punched a few numbers, and excused himself outside. Brooke glanced down at the outside camera monitors, watching the director when Tyler came into view on the camera in the hallway. Patrick saw her at the same time.

"I'll go get her."

Brooke nodded. She couldn't bear to look away, even for a moment.

❖

"So what's your plan?"

Carlson stopped pacing and pointed the gun at Styles.

"You. You're my plan. I'm going to use you as a hostage to get out of here."

Styles narrowed her eyes. "Really? You don't think that coming clean and surrendering at this point is a better alternative? You want to add kidnapping and hostage taking? Okay."

He growled in frustration and Jennifer whispered, "Stop. You're agitating him, and it's making it worse."

Styles whispered back, "I know what I'm doing."

Carlson walked up and punched Styles directly in the face, causing blood to gush from her nose and for her to double over. "I told you to shut up!"

❖

Brooke ran her hands through her hair in frustration. "He is starting to lose it. What the hell is she thinking? She's just making him more upset!"

Tyler walked up behind her. "No, she's keeping the attention on her, ensuring that she's the recipient of any frustration, and not Jennifer or Nicole."

Brooke placed her hands on the table. "We can't just sit here and do nothing."

The director walked back into the room. "I know what he was after." They all turned and looked. "We have a closed network computer system that houses hundreds of thousands of files. Those files contain the names and locations of not only clandestine operatives but of their contacts as well. This includes safe houses, known associates, and family members. Also, those computers house every single emergency scenario response plan for all branches of the government."

Tyler shook her head. "How do you know that?"

"We were finally able to trace those phone calls that you were receiving. It took a while because they were being rerouted all over the world and you only received two. Luckily, we caught a break and the caller left a tracer, clearly hoping to be found. When the FBI got to the actual location of origin, it was a woman's apartment. They found her dead inside, but she had left an encrypted file, detailing all of the elements of a thumb drive she had created. My best guess is that she was blackmailed into making it and so she was doing her best to get the people that she was being forced to work for caught, without putting herself in any imminent danger. I don't know if they actually ever figured out what she did, but they decided to eliminate her anyway."

Tyler rubbed her face. "Jesus Christ. You really could change the world with access to that type of information. If only we had found her sooner, maybe we could have done something to help her."

Kyle continued to stare at the monitors. "What do you think the likelihood is that Carlson knows who Thompson is working for?"

Tyler shook her head. "It's hard to say at this point."

The director hung up his phone again. "We have a team ready to break down the door and get them out."

Tyler glanced at Brooke before she spoke. "You can't do

that. He's unstable and he'll panic. Break down the door and you'll lose lives." The director waited for her to continue. "Let me go in and talk him down."

"Absolutely not," the director protested. "You aren't cleared for duty. I can't take that risk."

Brooke was still staring at the screen. "I can do it."

Kyle came back into the room with two other men, a variety of weapons in containers being towed behind them. Brooke glanced over. "But I'm not taking a weapon."

"The hell you aren't!" Tyler said.

Brooke turned to face her. "I can't go in there and talk him down if I'm armed. Besides, he's going to search me as soon as I walk in, and if he finds a weapon, it will break any trust I may be able to build."

Kyle turned away from the screens. "She's right. She needs to go in unarmed."

Tyler sat down, looking decidedly disgruntled. The director nodded. "I don't see any other alternative. Hart was in his class and his team leader. He'll listen to her before anyone else."

Tyler crossed her arms, staring at the monitors. "Be careful. If he starts to become volatile…"

Brooke was already headed to the door, but she waited for Tyler to finish.

"Just be careful." Tyler glanced at her and back to the monitors, her jaw clenching.

She gave Tyler one last smile and focused on what she needed to do. She knocked before she opened the door, her pulse pounding and her heart racing so hard she hoped she didn't faint or something stupid.

"Get out of here! I'll kill them all, I swear it!" The response was screamed from the other side of the wall, panic clear in the tone.

Brooke took a deep breath and entered the room with her hands in the air.

Carlson was immediately next to her, gun in her face. "What are you doing here?" His voice was shaking, full of emotion and fear.

"I wanted to come and talk to you, to help you."

He shook his head. "You can't help me now. No one can help me."

Brooke braved another step forward, wanting to get into the room to assess the situation for herself. "That's not true. I'm here to help."

Agitated, he pushed back. "Don't come any closer."

Brooke walked past him and leaned against one of the desks, so she could keep Carlson on one side and Nicole, Styles, and Jennifer on the other. If they were able to time it right, they could take him down easily. She quickly glanced over at the other three women, hoping they were thinking the same thing.

"I didn't know what was going to happen with the sergeant. I didn't know he was after her, Brooke." He almost sounded like he was whining.

Brooke nodded reassuringly. "I know. It's okay. Why don't you give me the gun and you can explain everything to the sergeant yourself."

"I don't need to give you my gun for that." He pointed the weapon at Brooke's head again. "She can hear everything I'm saying. You don't think I'm that dumb, do you?"

Brooke shook her head, waiting for the right moment.

❖

The director's phone rang again, and he moved away from the monitors.

Tyler was riveted to the screens, the worst possible scenarios flashing through her mind second by second.

Broadus closed the phone. "Thompson just killed himself." There was no emotion in his voice. He may as well have just said that it was raining outside. "He beat his head against the cell wall until he passed out, or what the guards thought was passed out when they reached him. Why the hell they weren't watching him…I'll find out. Anyway, we won't know for sure until they open him up, but the doctor assumes a massive brain bleed. Apparently, he decided death was better than talking."

Tyler continued to stare at the screen silently. As far as Tyler was concerned, he was better off dead. They were all better off with a maniac like him gone. The only downside was that he hadn't given them the name of the people he'd been working with, and they still didn't know how much information was out there. At the moment, though, her only concern was that Brooke and the others got out of that room safely.

❖

Styles made a forward circle motion with her hands, and Brooke assumed she wanted her to get Carlson talking. "Why did you really agree to help Thompson out?"

Carlson stood up straighter. "For the money. I already told them that." He pointed back to his other three captives.

"Yeah, and I believed you at first. Now I'm not so sure. I think you're playing dumb."

His grip tightened around the gun. His breathing became visually labored. He stared at her with wide eyes, his lips a tight white line.

"See, no one just throws all of this time, training, and energy away for money. If you were interested in money, you would have taken a position with a private firm where you could have made millions of dollars without this kind of hassle." Brooke hoped Patrick was on the other side of the wall, following this idea with research. She continued fishing, hoping she'd get him riled enough he'd lose focus. "I think you were placed here, on purpose, to do exactly what you did. What you didn't count on was Thompson going off plan because of the sergeant, and now you're trying to play catch-up."

He clicked off the safety and pointed it at Brooke's head. "Shut up."

❖

Everyone was looking over Patrick's shoulder.

"There." He pointed to the screen. "It says his parents are deceased, and at first glance, it seems to be true. There are death certificates, and he was living with a relative from nine years old on. However, when you double-check his birth certificate, the father's name is different, as is the place he was born. Brooke's right. Something is off."

Director Broadus shook his head. "How did this get missed?"

Patrick looked over. "Because there would be no reason to check it. The rest of his file is immaculate. But look who his father is…the one listed on his real birth certificate."

Nathaniel Lark: wanted by the FBI, CIA, and DEA for suspected terrorism and drug cartel connections.

Broadus turned to make another phone call, this time barking orders about doing a proper background check and finding out who the hell Carlson really was.

Tyler looked at the monitor, her only connection to Brooke. She closed her eyes and drew in a deep breath. If Brooke was right, there was more at stake than a recruit with bad decision-making skills. They were playing a game, but they didn't know the players or the rules. Somehow, he'd infiltrated one of the most secretive intelligence agencies in the world, and no one had noticed until he'd taken hostages. *Brooke. He's got Brooke.* She wanted more than anything to storm the room, to throw herself in front of Brooke and keep her safe. Instead, she had to watch the woman she loved face down a gun. She thought she might vomit.

Kyle came up beside her. "She is going to get out of this. They all are."

She realized the woman he loved was also a hostage. She squeezed his shoulder and nodded. "They all are. And then we'll get the truth. No matter what it takes."

❖

Brooke looked at the barrel of the gun, which she realized she had done more of in the past several days than she ever imagined she would in her whole life. "Who sent you?"

Carlson shook his head. "I can't tell if you're brave or stupid, Hart."

Styles said, "I would say a little bit of both."

He ignored her. "I didn't want to have to do this, Hart. I didn't want to have to kill you." He shrugged, the panic gone from his voice, and in its place an unnerving confidence. "But honestly, you've left me no choice. I can't have you spouting all kinds of things to make these other morons think, can I?" His jaw clenched. "And since you haven't fallen for my witless drama, at least I'll get to take one of you out before they take me away. Small consolation, but I'll take it." He leveled the gun at Brooke's head.

Brooke saw the movement happening behind him and kept

her eyes locked on his. "You always have a choice, Chris... and you're choosing to be an asshole."

As she was finishing her sentence, Glass kicked him in the side of the knee, and he stumbled forward. A follow-up roundhouse kick to the face, and he dropped the gun. It slid across the floor. He knelt, holding his head, with blood coming from his lip and eye. Brooke grabbed the gun, and Styles pushed him onto the ground, her knee in his back, and she placed zip ties around his wrists.

Glass said, "Zip ties, really?"

Styles pulled Carlson up and shrugged. "My handcuffs are in the office."

Brooke laughed. "And you just happen to have zip ties on you?"

Styles grinned. "What else does a girl keep in her pockets? You never know when you'll need to tie someone up, do you?"

The door swung open and person after person came rushing in.

The director reached Carlson first. "You and your father will never see another daylight hour."

Carlson spit on the floor next to his feet. "Everything would have gone perfectly if that idiot Thompson hadn't been so fucking obsessed with Monroe! I would have gotten the information. I would have given it to him, and everything would have been exactly the way we planned! I should have been the hero!"

"Get him out of here." Two heavily armed men dragged him out of the room.

He stopped and looked over his shoulder at Brooke. "I should have killed you when I had the chance, if only for my own satisfaction, you know-it-all, self-righteous bitch. You won't stop him, you know. There's nothing that you can do!"

Tyler was immediately next to Brooke. She hugged her,

and Brooke could feel the desperation in her embrace. She whispered into her ear, "I'm okay, honey. Everything is okay."

Tyler swallowed hard and straightened. "You did a great job, Jennifer. That was a perfect takedown."

"Thank you, ma'am."

Brooke shook her head. "Don't take this the wrong way, Glass, but if I had to have guessed who the insider was, my money would have been on you."

Jennifer raised an eyebrow. "Why me?"

Styles put her hand on her shoulder. "Because you can be, how can I put this…difficult to work with."

Jennifer pushed her hand away. "I don't understand how that makes me look guilty. I'm just focused."

"And generally miserable." Styles crossed her arms but didn't move away when Jennifer glared at her.

"I am not! You're the miserable one! I've never heard you even say anything resembling a joke until today, and your timing was horrible!"

"Things can change so fast," Brooke said to no one in particular. Nods of agreement validated her thought process.

Patrick came back into the room and handed the director several different printouts. "I got him. I know where we can find him."

Broadus patted him on the back. "Excellent work, Bowing."

Brooke asked, "What's going on?"

Kyle waved them toward the door. "Let's get out of here. We'll fill all of you in, but I need a drink."

Chapter Seventeen

Brooke and Tyler stood at the curb, hugging Claire good-bye.

"Please don't be a stranger, Tyler." Claire had her hand on Tyler's face, clearly trying to fight back her tears.

"I won't. I'm stateside now, so I'll be around much more often."

Brooke hugged her again before slipping her arms around Tyler's waist. "I'll make sure of it."

Claire got into the driver's seat and shut the door, waving as she drove away.

Brooke sighed. "She's wonderful."

Tyler looked at Brooke, who still had her arms wrapped around Tyler's waist. "Yes, she is. And so are you." They waited on the sidewalk until the car was completely out of sight.

Once inside, Tyler watched Brooke continue to pack her things meticulously into several different suitcases. "At least you'll still be with Patrick and Jennifer."

Brooke sighed. "I hate that I have to leave you. Have you heard anything?"

Tyler shook her head. "No, but I'm not even officially discharged yet." She started pulling at the strings on the comforter, watching them unravel, and wondered if her life was about to do the same.

"It's a medical discharge, Tyler. You completed your duty."

"I know. I'm just not sure what the next step is."

Brooke came around the bed and took her face with both hands. "You'll figure it out. We can do it together."

Tyler leaned into the touch. "Thank you."

There was a knock at the door, and Brooke opened the door to Patrick.

"I'm not interrupting, am I?"

Brooke walked back around to the other side of the bed and continued to pack. "No, come on in."

He took a seat at the empty desk in the corner of the room. "I just talked to Agent Styles. They have a lead on Lark. He's been running an anti-American terrorist organization for the last several years under the cloak of an investing firm. They went to pick him up, but he's in the wind. Styles said they're working on tracking him down, but with his money and connections it's going to be a bitch to find him."

Tyler shook her head. "I still can't believe that Carlson... or I guess his real last name is Lark, was a part of all this and I had no idea. I feel like I should have seen it during training."

Brooke stopped her folding and looked at Tyler for a long moment before saying anything. "Do you ever stop beating yourself up for things you can't control? Not even the CIA figured it out until it was almost too late. You're only one person, Tyler. Don't be so hard on yourself."

Jennifer entered the room, smiling bigger than Tyler had ever seen. "I can't believe that we're all going to share an apartment together!" She paused briefly, seemingly in rather deep thought. "To think, I spent a whole year despising your existence, Hart."

Brooke rolled her eyes. "Yeah. It only took two life-threatening situations and seven shots of vodka to make you bearable."

Jennifer rolled her eyes. "Ha ha." She moved her suitcase around so she could sit. "I told you I was sorry. I have trouble assimilating and I'm highly competitive. It's a terrible combination. You were always better at damn near everything, and it pissed me off. Sorry."

Brooke smiled at her. "You can stop apologizing. We're moving forward with a clean slate. But from now on, I'm going to call you on it when you get bitchy." She pulled one of her suitcases over to the door and changed the subject. She had told Tyler that she wanted to be friends with Jennifer, and was going to avoid rehashing their tension over and over. "I can't believe we were all placed in Clandestine Services. That normally takes years."

Tyler stared out the window. "Well, you all earned it. Think about what you prevented. They would be stupid to place you anywhere else." The sun was just starting to set, nighttime was crashing down, and Brooke would be leaving for her new, prestigious post in the CIA. She mindlessly moved her leg up and down, enjoying the stretching motion, although she wondered how much longer the dull pain would be there. Her phone rang. She glanced at the caller ID and moved away slightly for privacy. "Monroe."

Tyler listened to the voice on the other end of the line while she watched as Brooke, Patrick, and Jennifer continued to talk amongst themselves—furniture types, paint colors, different styles of décor for their new place. Patrick dramatically clutched at his heart. "What have I gotten myself into?"

Tyler ended her call and looked at Brooke, motioning slightly with her head.

She stopped packing and walked over to Tyler. "What is it?"

Tyler kissed her on the cheek, grabbed her keys and jacket, and said, "I have to go to a meeting. I'll call you later. Drive safe."

"Can't tell me any more than that?"

Tyler shook her head but gave Brooke a lingering kiss, ignoring the silly catcalls from the other two. "Not yet. But I'll tell you when I can. I'll call you as soon as I'm done." She left, glad she was able to go before Brooke finished packing. Watching that and knowing she'd soon be alone again was tearing her up. She'd been on her own for so long, but now the thought of being without Brooke made her ache inside. She tossed her crutches onto the passenger seat and pulled out of the driveway, the lump in her throat making it hard to swallow back the tears.

As she headed to her meeting, she prayed this might offer a solution.

❖

Tyler waited in the lobby and concentrated on the floor lined with stark white tiles, with the emblem of the United States of America shining in bright blue slates. She watched people come and go in suits, carrying briefcases. She realized how far out of her element she really was. The only thing she ever carried to work was a rifle, and a tie would look ridiculous with her BDUs. *And my crutches.*

Agent Styles came out from behind a sliding glass door, talking on the phone, and when she saw Tyler, she motioned her over. She hung up and led the way down another hallway. "I'm sorry for keeping you waiting. The idiot at the counter didn't let me know you'd arrived."

"It's not a problem."

They made a left turn down a hallway. Through clear office doors, Tyler saw people hurrying about, phones ringing everywhere, and she thought the place resembled newsrooms she had seen in the movies. *A newsroom all about bad guys.*

"How are your leg and side feeling?"

"Much better. I should be able to start running again in a month or so. I've been sticking to swimming laps per the doctors' orders, like a good little patient. I won't use a wheelchair, but the crutches work."

"I'm sure that has far more to do with Analyst Hart's orders than those of any doctor."

Tyler smiled. "True story."

They entered an enormous conference room, with a table that looked large enough to sit twenty people, but it was just the two of them inside.

"I apologize. This room seems overwhelming, but it was the only available space."

Tyler took a seat and waited for Styles to do the same. She seemed far more relaxed than she had a few months ago. "Agent, what is—"

"Call me Caden, please."

"Okay, what's up, Caden? Why couldn't you talk to me over the phone?"

Styles swiveled back and forth in her chair, tapping a pen to her cheek. "I want to offer you a job."

Tyler was surprised. She'd thought it would have to do with the open case. "You do? Not even the Marine Corps wants me anymore."

Styles grinned. "The Marine Corps aren't necessarily known for their brilliant decision-making capabilities." She paused, amused at Tyler's glare. "Listen, I've seen you work. I've read all your files. I know that you're honorable, demand respect, and have the highest level of integrity. I can't think of any other qualifications you would need. Unless you want to stay at the Farm? Do you like being a training officer?"

Tyler looked down, always embarrassed by compliments. "I don't know, really. The Farm was kind of an intermediary step while I waited for my medical discharge. I hadn't planned beyond it. What would you like me to do?"

"I want you to come work for me in our Anti-Terrorism Task Force here in D.C."

She said it so plainly, she may as well had been telling Tyler to pick up milk from the store. "Wow. That's a huge compliment. Thank you for considering me."

Styles stood up. "Perfect, let's get to work."

Tyler raised her hand to stop her. "I have to talk to Brooke first."

"Right. I figured as much." Styles pulled out an envelope from her pocket and handed it to Tyler. "Here's all the information about the job—salary, benefits, you know, the normal stuff. There's also a hotel key in there. We booked you a room for a week at the Liaison, so you can get some thinking room away from the Farm. If you decide to take the job, I know some great apartments around here. I can help you get set up."

Tyler took the envelope, glad her hands weren't shaking with excitement. "Caden, really, thank you. I'll get back to you as soon as possible."

Styles shook her hand. "I'm counting on it. I would really like your help with Lark, and I'm pretty sure you'd like a crack at him too."

Tyler followed her out of the large hallway and into the front lobby. They said their good-byes and Tyler continued to the large parking structure. She'd broken down and bought herself a little beat-up car, and as she approached, she saw a familiar figure leaning against the trunk. "Brooke? What are you doing here? How did you know I was here?"

Brooke poked her in the chest. "The question is, what are you doing here?"

Tyler was still confused. "Did you trace my phone?"

Brooke shrugged. "You didn't answer my question."

Tyler leaned against the trunk and crossed her arms. "You could have just called me...or texted me...or anything but run a trace on my phone."

"You were acting all secretive. I got worried." It was clear by the tone in Brooke's voice she realized she was in the wrong.

"Because I didn't know why they wanted me down here. Do you honestly think I would leave you in the dark if I knew what was going on?"

Brooke seemed to consider for a moment. "All valid points."

Tyler sighed and rubbed her temples. "Where is your car?"

Brooke was kicking at nothing, another nervous habit Tyler usually found adorable. "I took a cab from the new apartment. It's actually pretty close."

Tyler leaned over, smiled, and kissed her. "Get in the car, crazy woman."

"I'm really sorry. I don't know what I was thinking. I kind of lost my mind. Working in intelligence makes you see ghosts everywhere. And with what we've been through, I guess I'm not handling it perfectly."

Tyler took her hand. "No, you aren't."

Brooke rolled her eyes. "So, what were you doing down here?"

Tyler kept looking straight ahead, maneuvering through the evening traffic. "Styles offered me a job. She wants me to work for her in the Anti-Terrorism Unit here in D.C."

Brooke jumped in her seat. "Tyler! That's wonderful! I'm so happy for you! That's the answer, right? To what to do now that you're not in the Marines?"

Tyler beamed at her, happy that Brooke seemed to want her around. "And Langley and D.C. are only ten miles apart. Now you really won't be able to get rid of me."

Brooke grabbed her hand and kissed her knuckles. "Tyler, I don't ever want to get rid of you."

Tyler's heart felt like it might jump from her chest, the words made her so euphoric. "So, I should take it, right?"

Brooke pushed her arm playfully. "Of course! Tyler, when we decided that you would move to this area and look for a job, I was secretly worried you would resent me for keeping you from something like moving back to North Carolina with your aunt. Or not being able to find a job that you really wanted to do. Now both of our dreams are coming true. I think it's fabulous."

Tyler pulled into the Liaison and parked the car. She turned and looked at Brooke. "Are you sure you're ready for all of this? For us?"

Brooke leaned over and kissed Tyler slowly, making a promise to her that didn't require words. "I have been ready for you my whole life. I want to love you forever, in any way you'll let me."

Tyler sank into the kiss, letting go of the past in the face of a future she couldn't have dreamed of. "Then let's go upstairs and start working on our forever."

About the Author

Jackie D was born and raised in the San Francisco, East Bay area of California, where she still resides. She earned a bachelor's degree in recreation administration and a dual master's degree in management and public administration. She is a Navy veteran and served in Operation Iraqi Freedom as a flight deck director on board the USS *Abraham Lincoln*. She spends her free time with her friends, family, and incredibly needy dogs. She enjoys playing golf but is resigned to the fact she would equally enjoy any sport where drinking beer is encouraged during game play. *Infiltration: Book One of the After Dark Series* is her first book. She is currently working on the sequel.

Jackie can be contacted at jackie_d1981@yahoo.com.

Books Available From Bold Strokes Books

Cold to the Touch by Cari Hunter. A drug addict's murder is the start of a dangerous investigation for Detective Sanne Jensen and Dr. Meg Fielding, as they try to stop a killer with no conscience. (978-1-62639-526-8)

Forsaken by Laydin Michaels. The hunt for a killer teaches one woman that she must overcome her fear in order to love, and another that success is meaningless without happiness. (978-1-62639-481-0)

Infiltration by Jackie D. When a CIA breach is imminent, a Marine instructor must stop the attack while protecting her heart from being disarmed by a recruit. (978-1-62639-521-3)

Midnight at the Orpheus by Alyssa Linn Palmer. Two women desperate to make their way in the world, a man hell-bent on revenge, and a cop risking his career: all in a day's work in Capone's Chicago. (978-1-62639-607-4)

Spirit of the Dance by Mardi Alexander. Major Sorla Reardon's return to her family farm to heal threatens Riley Johnson's safe life when small-town secrets are revealed, and love may not conquer all. (978-1-62639-583-1)

Sweet Hearts by Melissa Brayden, Rachel Spangler, and Karis Walsh. Do you ever wonder *Whatever happened to...*? Find out when you reconnect with your favorite characters from Melissa Brayden's *Heart Block*, Rachel Spangler's *LoveLife*, and Karis Walsh's *Worth the Risk*. (978-1-62639-475-9)

Totally Worth It by Maggie Cummings. Who knew there's an all-lesbian condo community in the NYC suburbs? Join twentysomething BFFs Meg and Lexi at Bay West as they navigate friendships, love, and everything in between. (978-1-62639-512-1)

Illicit Artifacts by Stevie Mikayne. Her foster mother's death cracked open a secret world Jil never wanted to see...and now she has to pick up the stolen pieces. (978-1-62639-472-8)

Pathfinder by Gun Brooke. Heading for their new homeworld, Exodus's chief engineer Adina Vantressa and nurse Briar Lindemay carry game-changing secrets that may well cause them to lose everything when disaster strikes. (978-1-62639-444-5)

Prescription for Love by Radclyffe. Dr. Flannery Rivers finds herself attracted to the new ER chief, city girl Abigail Remy, and the incendiary mix of city and country, fire and ice, tradition and change is combustible. (978-1-62639-570-1)

Ready or Not by Melissa Brayden. Uptight Mallory Spencer finds relinquishing control to bartender Hope Sanders too tall an order in fast-paced New York City. (978-1-62639-443-8)

Summer Passion by MJ Williamz. Women loving women is forbidden in 1946 Hollywood, yet Jean and Maggie strive to keep their love alive and away from prying eyes. (978-1-62639-540-4)

The Princess and the Prix by Nell Stark. "Ugly duckling" Princess Alix of Monaco was resigned to loneliness until she met racecar driver Thalia d'Angelis. (978-1-62639-474-2)

Winter's Harbor by Aurora Rey. Lia Brooks isn't looking for love in Provincetown, but when she discovers chocolate croissants and pastry chef Alex McKinnon, her winter retreat quickly starts heating up. (978-1-62639-498-8)

The Time Before Now by Missouri Vaun. Vivian flees a disastrous affair, embarking on an epic, transformative journey to escape her past, until destiny introduces her to Ida, who helps her rediscover trust, love, and hope. (978-1-62639-446-9)

Twisted Whispers by Sheri Lewis Wohl. Betrayal, lies, and secrets—whispers of a friend lost to darkness. Can a reluctant psychic set things right or will an evil soul destroy those she loves? (978-1-62639-439-1)

The Courage to Try by C.A. Popovich. Finding love is worth getting past the fear of trying. (978-1-62639-528-2)

Break Point by Yolanda Wallace. In a world readying for war, can love find a way? (978-1-62639-568-8)

Countdown by Julie Cannon. Can two strong-willed, powerful women overcome their differences to save the lives of seven others and begin a life they never imagined together? (978-1-62639-471-1)

Keep Hold by Michelle Grubb. Claire knew some things should be left alone and some rules should never be broken, but the most forbidden, well, they are the most tempting. (978-1-62639-502-2)

Deadly Medicine by Jaime Maddox. Dr. Ward Thrasher's life is in turmoil. Her partner Jess left her, and her job puts her in the path of a murderous physician who has Jess in his sights. (978-1-62639-424-7)

New Beginnings by KC Richardson. Can the connection and attraction between Jordan Roberts and Kirsten Murphy be enough for Jordan to trust Kirsten with her heart? (978-1-62639-450-6)

Officer Down by Erin Dutton. Can two women who've made careers out of being there for others in crisis find the strength to need each other? (978-1-62639-423-0)

Reasonable Doubt by Carsen Taite. Just when Sarah and Ellery think they've left dangerous careers behind, a new case sets them—and their hearts—on a collision course. (978-1-62639-442-1)

Tarnished Gold by Ann Aptaker. Cantor Gold must outsmart the Law, outrun New York's dockside gangsters, outplay a shady art dealer, his lover, and a beautiful curator, and stay out of a killer's gun sights. (978-1-62639-426-1)

White Horse in Winter by Franci McMahon. Love between two women collides with the inner poison of a closeted horse trainer in the green hills of Vermont. (978-1-62639-429-2)

Autumn Spring by Shelley Thrasher. Can Bree and Linda, two women in the autumn of their lives, put their hearts first and find the love they've never dared seize? (978-1-62639-365-3)

The Renegade by Amy Dunne. Post-apocalyptic survivors Alex and Evelyn secretly find love while held captive by a deranged cult, but when their relationship is discovered, they must fight for their freedom—or die trying. (978-1-62639-427-8)

Thrall by Barbara Ann Wright. Four women in a warrior society must work together to lift an insidious curse while caught between their own desires, the will of their peoples, and an ancient evil. (978-1-62639-437-7)

The Chameleon's Tale by Andrea Bramhall. Two old friends must work through a web of lies and deceit to find themselves again, but in the search they discover far more than they ever went looking for. (978-1-62639-363-9)

Side Effects by VK Powell. Detective Jordan Bishop and Dr. Neela Sahjani must decide if it's easier to trust someone with your heart or your life as they face threatening protestors, corrupt politicians, and their increasing attraction. (978-1-62639-364-6)

Warm November by Kathleen Knowles. What do you do if the one woman you want is the only one you can't have? (978-1-62639-366-0)

In Every Cloud by Tina Michele. When Bree finally leaves her shattered life behind, is she strong enough to salvage the remaining pieces of her heart and find the place where it truly fits? (978-1-62639-413-1)

Rise of the Gorgon by Tanai Walker. When independent Internet journalist Elle Pharell goes to Kuwait to investigate a veteran's mysterious suicide, she hires Cassandra Hunt, an interpreter with a covert agenda. (978-1-62639-367-7)

Crossed by Meredith Doench. Agent Luce Hansen returns home to catch a killer and risks everything to revisit the unsolved murder of her first girlfriend and confront the demons of her youth. (978-1-62639-361-5)

Making a Comeback by Julie Blair. Music and love take center stage when jazz pianist Liz Randall tries to make a comeback with the help of her reclusive, blind neighbor, Jac Winters. (978-1-62639-357-8)

Soul Unique by Gun Brooke. Self-proclaimed cynic Greer Landon falls for Hayden Rowe's paintings and the young woman shortly after, but will Hayden, who lives with Asperger syndrome, trust her and reciprocate her feelings? (978-1-62639-358-5)

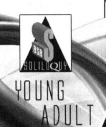